DogFellow's Ghost

GAVIN SMITH

DogFellow's Ghost

Macmillan New Writing

First published 2008 by Macmillan New Writing
an imprint of Pan Macmillan Ltd
Pan Macmillan, 20 New Wharf Road, London N1 9RR
Basingstoke and Oxford
Associated companies throughout the world
www.panmacmillan.com

ISBN 978-0-330-46099-6

1 3 5 7 9 8 6 4 2

A CIP catalogue record for this book is available
from the British Library.

Typeset by Intype Libra, London
Printed and bound in UK by
MPG Books Ltd, Bodmin, Cornwall

For my parents,
Trevor and Valerie Smith

His name was DogFellow and he walked awkwardly along the dirt track that cut across the island's southern tip. It was early afternoon and powerfully warm, making him pant hard, with his tongue half out of his mouth. He sweated too, although not much – just enough to dampen the coarse grey hair that shadowed his back and ran in a deep V from the rise of his sternum down to his navel.

When he looked through the trees he could make out the unending ocean, its surface brilliant and sparkling with a million flakes of light. Yet he was unmoved by the spectacle and passed on his way, along the skirt of the shore to where the ruins of the house were to be found. Already he might glimpse the crumbling walls, in all their mottled ugliness. He could see how the roof had caved in, and the way in which the surrounding palisade had been beaten flat. He stopped, as if to survey the catastrophe: but it was not this which had drawn him. He knew well enough how fast things decayed in the tropical swelter, how sudden storms would come raging out of the sea, with monstrous winds and overbearing waves. His attention was given only to the windows that once had white shutters for lids, but now were blind, the glass put out. At these he looked and waited, waited a long time, staring at the dark blind holes as if anticipating a movement or sign from within.

He was almost lost in a trance. He muttered to himself, saying what might be a nonsensical chant or a half-formed prayer. Then, all at once, he paused. He heard something – someone – moving in the tangle of brush to his right. His hearing was wonderfully acute.

'DogFellow?'

Quivering with guilty surprise, with a heartsick fear, he spied Slope regarding him from behind a veil of leaves and was at once relieved: poor Slope, the least considered and the most trusting of all the beast people. There came the crackle of twigs as Slope climbed from his nest.

'DogFellow, you come talk with me?'

DogFellow did not know why he had walked this way. He nodded, blinking back the spectre of tears.

'We go down to the water?'

He watched as Slope shambled over. He was perplexed that anyone could abandon the huts and come to live in such a place. Slope's coarse, ill-made hand paddled against his own.

'We go now?'

He noticed – as if it were for the first time – the terrible raised welts that ran down on either side of Slope's jaw, so stark and pronounced that no hair could ever grow back there. He noticed, too, Slope's tiny eyes of absolute

and unvaried blackness and the sorry flaps of skin that had
been teased into an approximation of man-ears.

'We go?'

Slope's tongue was thick and clumsy, his words slurred
and sometimes drowned in the mouth.

'Go catch shrimp, DogFellow?'

DogFellow set his own hand on to Slope's lumpish
shoulder.

'Yes. We can go and catch. But not here. It is better to
go on to the tumbled rocks. There is no good catching of
shrimps by this place.'

So together they turned about and walked to where the
ground was easier, past an old banyan tree that was
broken-backed with age and then out from the lee of the
forest and on to the sand.

The tumbled rocks DogFellow spoke of lay like a bar-
rier across the beach, blocking out all views of the house,
although he briefly strained about and tried to look:
hoping, fearing. Slope, untroubled, waddled towards the
sea, raising his long arms as if he were balancing on a
beam.

The Pacific hissed and sighed. They felt the sand cool
and dampen. Suddenly the outer froth of the surf rode over
their toes, tickling deliciously.

'We catch shrimp?' repeated Slope tirelessly.

'We catch them now,' replied DogFellow.

They started to wade out into the shallows until
DogFellow was up to his knees and Slope thigh deep. The
water bore the slightest green-blue tincture, and darting
through it was the prey they were after. Soon DogFellow,

3

using his hands as a trap, had pulled out over a dozen, and he gave them to Slope, who held his tatty shirt hem out.

When they had caught enough they walked back up the strand and sat down, enjoying the shade. Together they consumed their trawl, nipping off the heads and spitting them out. As he ate, DogFellow considered how the nails on his hands were getting overlong. A light breeze came off the sea. Slope yawned and stretched, giving a little shudder of pleasure. After a while DogFellow could not help but ask, 'Last time and the time before, when we gather to say the things the Master told us, I did not see you there. Why was that? Were you sick?'

Slope did not answer, yet something approximating a frown creased his broad and bulbous forehead.

'We were all there. All except you,' continued Dog Fellow, though this was very far from being true. 'Just because the Master has gone away does not mean we must forget the Law – what you been doing anyhow?'

But still Slope made no reply. The faint suggestion of perplexity had passed, like a shadow flitting across the sea. The shadow had passed and the sea abided, immeasurably calm, unfathomably void. DogFellow did not press further. He understood that there was no guile beneath the surface. The simple truth was that Slope had forgotten much.

'Hey!'

The cry, sudden and sharp, brought DogFellow to his senses. He had left Slope and walked back up from the

4

beach, the fishy flavour of shrimps still on his lips. Now he studied the spaces between the trees, thinking he saw a vine tremble, and with hands on hips he said, 'Who hides? Friend or foe?'

'Friend!'

The word seemed to issue from behind a hefty tree trunk, but as he tried to peer a morsel of stone whisked from out of the shadows and caught DogFellow below the right ear.

'Foe!'

With a grunt of annoyance he began to walk away, but had not managed four or five paces before there was the sound of running and Lemura was beside him, his pale face set in a grin.

'Did you guess me?'

'Yes,' he replied, without breaking his stride.

'Ah, you lie. DogFellow's a sly one. It is sly to lie. Hey –'

This time Lemura's shapely fingers tapped DogFellow on the forearm.

'What do you want?'

'I know a secret.'

Lemura's mouth puckered into a conceited smile. His eyes glowed with amusement. The skin of his chin and cheeks was naturally smooth and unmarked by the knife.

'Good,' said DogFellow. 'I hope it brings you happiness.'

Pretending not to be drawn, he took to observing the way the light slanted through the tent of branches over their heads.

'Be good, be good; be good in the wood,' chanted Lemura. Then he said, 'I tell you, DogFellow. Stop and sit by me.'

'This had better not be one of your games.'

'Oh?'

'If you are trying to trick me I'll bite you – understand?'

He curled back his lip to bring home the point, baring his teeth.

'Ahhh!' exclaimed Lemura. 'Fierce, fierce!'

'Fierce and fast. So no tricks. We agree?'

'No tricks. I tell you true. I give you secret.'

Suddenly Lemura's smile had gone and he was staring earnestly into DogFellow's face. Together they went and squatted on a log.

'So?' said DogFellow.

'A secret, a secret, who can keep it?'

'I warn you –'

Lemura nodded, saying, 'Yes, yes. I tell you now. Last night, last night – do you know about last night? It was dark. Except the moon. It was big. Big in my eye, so I could not sleep. He looks down and watches me. I watch him back, on and on. I waited for him to blink.'

'The moon does not blink.'

'Yes, yes,' said Lemura. 'Now I know that. But then I hear a noise.'

'What kind of noise?'

'Like when the sea talks. But not the same. And another noise comes, and another, louder and louder. You understand?'

6

DogFellow frowned.

'Did you go and look?'

'I was already sitting out, on the high cliff just there. At first, nothing. But then I can tell there are others –'

'Other beast people?'

Lemura nodded, as if wary.

'Tell me. How many were there?'

Here his grin returned, now founded upon embarrassment.

'Two,' he said.

'Who were they?'

Lemura did not answer for a moment. Then he said, 'Fantine and Hector.'

DogFellow's expression changed.

'Did they see you?'

'No,' said Lemura.

'But you saw them?'

'I watch them. I watch them so long I get an ache down all my side.'

'What were they doing?'

Lemura snorted and averted his face. Without looking about he said, 'Badness.'

'What do you mean? What badness? Tell me.'

'The worst of the forbidden things.'

'The worst . . .?'

'Yes.'

'The very worst?'

'Yes. That which the Master told we must never do.'

'You did not mistake this?'

'No,' said Lemura, shaking his head.

7

'Who else have you told?'

'Only you, DogFellow. You know about the forbidden things. The Master, he teach you better than best. Better than any other beast person.'

DogFellow was not flattered to hear this. He was hardly listening. He considered the gravity of the accusation, the iniquity of the crime. Then, without knowing what to do, he swore Lemura to silence, and so they parted.

Later, and DogFellow was sitting alone in his hut. Outside the late afternoon sun poured down its bounty. Through various cracks and fissures in the roof the light seeped in, falling across his outstretched legs. He watched the circular play of dust motes until a residual thirstiness left over from his salty dinner got him up on to his haunches to slop water from his battered jug into a tin cup. He noticed again how awkward his nails were becoming. Carefully, as he had been taught, he raised the cup to his lips and sipped, letting the water trickle into his mouth. He gulped and continued until the cup was empty. He wiped the droplets from his chin with the back of his hand and tried to settle himself. But then he heard the scuff of feet and a voice raised in salutation. Who could be coming, at this time? The voice called again and he realized with a sick lurch that it was Hector. As quick as he could he went to pull the sackcloth curtain down across his doorway. He was already too late. Hector stood outside, observing DogFellow with his familiar, friendly stare. There was not even the suspicion of shame.

'How is it, old chap?' he asked. 'Are you napping?'
DogFellow, hardly daring to respond, simply shrugged.
'You want to eat a little?'

'I am not hungry.'

'I got plenty,' continued Hector, as if he had not
heard, and he held up a stem with a cluster of unripe
bananas attached. DogFellow glanced from the fruit to
the face, so like his own – the same suture creases, the
same thin lips and queer nose; and he tried to imagine
Hector in some lewd forbidden posture, panting and
thrusting, with Fantine's own mouth stretched as wide as
her legs.

'I am not hungry,' he repeated, his voice flat.

'Are you poorly?'

'Yes, sick,' said DogFellow. 'My stomach hurts. Just
here.'

He pressed one finger to the middle of his belly, where
the hair was especially thick and curly.

'Oh ho,' said Hector and peered, as if he might diag-
nose the pain just as the Master could. He said, 'Go to
where the springs are, and dig a little earth. Swallow it
down quick. I help you –'

'No,' said DogFellow, drawing back, even as Hector
would reach out and take his hand.

'All right, DogFellow,' said Hector, his good humour
unshakeable. 'But earth from the springs – it is good for
the belly. Makes the hurt better in double-quick time.
Don't forget!'

He grinned lopsidedly and with a funny roll of the
shoulders he turned and went away. His gait mirrored

DogFellow's own, except he had no limp. DogFellow watched him, seeing how he took the path back to the forest, away from the huts, and then he tugged at the ragged hem of the door-flap, letting the piece of sacking fall.

He was alone again, amidst the shadows and the shafts of afternoon light. Perhaps Lemura was mistaken. Perhaps there was no Hector, no Fantine, and no midnight deed, done beneath the moon or in darkness. And yet he allowed himself to imagine it performed, and he could not turn his face against the thought. He tried to evade it through lying down on his bed and shutting his eyes. He was always punctilious in how he went about this: stretching out like a stick of wood, with his ugly misshapen feet poking out from under the bottom end of the blanket. He slept like a man, on his back, and not curled up. He set his hands on top of the cover, palms down. He closed his eyes and waited.

Time passed, and the thought was still there, a thought-picture, projecting like an image from a magic lantern on to the underside of his lids. He groaned and wished it away, remembering the words of the Law, remembering the words of the Master. Could He hear him now, as he called out?

The image he saw jumped, blurred, became something else.

Without realizing, DogFellow fell asleep.

He awoke to perfect darkness, trembling as if the fever had hold of him.

For several moments he was abjectly befuddled, remembering nothing about anything, and then in a rush the knowledge came back to him, racing across the flatlands of his mind and foaming upwards until his head was filled almost to bursting. He struggled to sit up, wrestling against the folds of the blanket, feeling the ache swell in his knees and the manic sprinting of his heart. He attempted to chase off the dread panic he felt by concentrating only on what was good, seeing only good things, and so he rolled on to his side and contrived to find what was hidden in his mattress, but what comfort could it give him, when he did not even have light enough to discover his hand in front of his face? In the dark, in despair, he got up and went to pull back the door-flap. He looked to the sky to find the famous moon, that saw all and told no one, but it had disappeared. Only the stars remained, stippling the blue-blackness. The air was soft and caressing and scented with the rich odour of tropical flowers. There were no sounds save for the faintest murmur from sea and forest, yet these were drowned out by DogFellow's laboured breathing. The bad pictures were there in front of him, the starkness undiminished, each image telling him it is not then: no, *it is still* now. *He saw again the locked door, the man who waits, the face all covered in blood, the bloody face that speaks his name. He shuddered convulsively, half recoiling, and, gripping the wooden strut that did service for a door frame, tried to straighten his legs, ignoring the sharp pain that followed.*

'But they will be punished,' he gasped, breathing his words out into the tropical night. 'Yes, they will be punished' – though he did not know how.

There was no one near to hear him speak. The beast people had left their huts and slept out among the trees.

One

The Master.

First of all, at the penumbra of consciousness, so vague and indistinct as to seem more like a dream, more physical sensation than visual image, he sees or rather smells a track between tall grass. Ahead there are bare legs running, and he runs too, with a grace and speed he can scarce believe. There are cries and shouts and his own excited voice booming out. Then: then there is a long emptiness, with only the loosest sense of one day being on a boat at sea and wandering the deck, while from below comes the hot stink of caged animals. But whether this is true remembrance or a dream he has had since he can't be sure. Only the shining blade and the words in the dark are indubitably real, for the Master spoke even as he cut, saying 'Good boy' and 'There's a lovely lad' and 'Shush now', this last always uttered as a benediction, and followed by a soft caress of the head as it lay in its iron bonnet. With one hand he sliced, with the other he smoothed, and always there came the voice, as deep and all-encompassing as the great Pacific itself.

DogFellow remembers leather straps buckled across his limbs – the legs that had become arms; the paws that were transfigured into hands – and the agony of his hips and spine, wrenched into verticality and hammered straight with steel pins. Yet worse, beyond every other grievance, was the knife set against the skull, scratching beneath rough shaved flesh, tearing flaps and severing muscle with pitiless exactitude. The mouth, the tongue, the throat, the palate, the muzzle, the teeth, the jaw beneath: all is broken, split and rendered down, the better to be made again. Then, lastly, the brain.

A third of the year went by. DogFellow knows this to be so for the Master told him, and who could doubt the word of the Master? For all that, the agony seems confined to a single, long night – two at most – and in the day between he recalls only scrubbed wooden boards and the giddying stench of chloroform, flavoured with his own blood. Then, at last, there is the morning that the Master wakes him with a gentle touch and bids him rise up and walk; and with pride and love watches as, so slowly, and with so much care, DogFellow struggles to sit.

The Master wears his shirtsleeves rolled, the whiteness of the cloth matching the whiteness of his forearms, scrubbed as smooth as marble. These arms are as hard as marble too, with the muscle dense and swelling, and the grip of his hands like the power of the sea. DogFellow squats on a low bench, his scars livid, his backbone braced. There are two beast people by him, equally marked up with fresh sutures, though by their heavy faces and lumpish bodies they reveal their former status as pigs: pigs, raised to men by the Master's craft. It is he who stands before them, admiring what he has done, and slowly says, 'Can you hear me?'

DogFellow nods with difficulty, for his neck is very sore. The pig-men look one to the other. The one nearest DogFellow emits a snuffle, which satisfies the Master, because he says, 'Good. You will listen, and through listening you will learn. Now, to begin: watch me and follow.'

They look as he points to his mouth and with a deal of grimacing pronounces the first sound they must repeat: the letter 'a'. He says it again and again, coaxing the beasts to utter it; and because they fear him and love him, each struggles to echo the noise, opening their still tender jaws and arching their stitched tongues in imitation. For a while DogFellow can only manage a wretched hawking, bringing the taste of blood into his mouth. The pig-men are caught up in a sequence of gruff nasal honks. The Master finally strides across and with one hand – the hand that cuts – catches at DogFellow's chin, drawing it down so that the pink and red of the mouth's interior is revealed.

'Now,' he says, his beard bearing the odour of tobacco, his breath richly freighted with scents. 'Do what I tell you.'

So frightened he fears he will lose consciousness, DogFellow pulls upward against the pressure of those steely fingers, humps the scarified hide of his tongue, tenses new muscle deep inside his chest, and manages a tortured, elongated but still recognizable cry of 'a'. '*Aaaaa*,' he goes. And again, '*Aaaaa*.'

'Excellent,' says the Master, and brushes the backs of his fingers across DogFellow's face. DogFellow's pain turns immediately to tremulous pleasure. He wants to lick at that hand, and cannot contain a low whine. Instantly the fingers which stroke are straightened and bat him across the bridge of the nose. 'No,' he is told; and the tremor that had excited DogFellow's non-existent tail is instantly stilled.

DogFellow sleeps on straw and sits at his bench. His scars grow pale and his mouth discovers new subtleties: how to break sealed lips and shape a 'b'; how to reseal the split and mould an 'm'. He discovers how some words are born when the tongue strikes the palate; and that others are conjured up in the back of the throat. He learns how to say 'Master'. He learns how to fathom the Master's moods. Shortly after, and he can tell the sea from the land, and the trees from the shore. What hitherto was only felt, in the inchoate realm of pure sense, is now exploded into a thousand shards, and every shard has its own shape, its own edges, and exists in the mind and in the mouth. Weeks pass and he begins to understand that the Master does not disappear into air when he leaves the room, but works elsewhere. Sometimes, beneath the odour of tobacco and the smell of strong soap, DogFellow can catch the reek of strange, unfamiliar beings. Sometimes at night he is roused to wakefulness by the screeching of some unknown thing.

The pig-men learn alongside him, but while he hobbles ahead, they drag behind on club feet. In everything he is quick, and an earnest seeker-out of praise. When the pig-men are presented with the hand mirror they balk, startled to see another brought into the room. Yet when he is shown he wrinkles his eyes and pulls back his upper lip, in imitation of the Master. And when the Master asks what he sees he at once replies.

He says, '*DogFellow*.'

Two

During the time before dawn there is movement among the huts where the beast people live. In the gloom only black shapes can be seen, which snort and grunt and shiver in the cool air. The loudest sound is the repetitive tramp of feet. DogFellow falls into line, following the shambling form which walks half a dozen yards in front of him. The forest is darker still, although the occasional shrill burst of birdsong breaks the stillness. The path alone seems possessed of a spectral glow. DogFellow runs behind a tree and pisses a stream, keeping both legs on the ground, as he has been taught. Even in the dark the Master can see everything.

He quickly moves back on to the path, trotting ahead until the forest thins and the noise of the sea insinuates itself in his cocked ear. The sand is dry and compact underfoot. By first light, which now breaks across the Pacific's inky flatness, he is able to see a string of bodies, already lined up. There are fifteen of them, which means – not counting DogFellow – another twelve have yet to come.

Some appear tall, rangy even; others combine height with bulk, and stand like small megaliths, their square heads slumped forward across broad and often massive shoulders. DogFellow is middle-sized. Stepping briskly, he joins the rank.

They must not speak, nor associate with one another, but out of the corner of his eye he studies the imposing profile of BearCreature, who is smacking his lips, as if he has already eaten breakfast. To his left Slope waddles forward and, sighing, stands to attention. In another few moments the full complement has assembled. A certain pinkishness – the colour of new scar tissue – begins to infect the eastern sky, though the windows in the Master's house remain as blank as slate. They all wait patiently. Perhaps he will have a new member for their society: it has been nearly five months since the ship last arrived, with its boxed and chained cargo, and there has been much hidden exertion, through the days and late into the night. Further down the line there is muttering. Lemura's high voice can be heard, and Handy's. Then, briefly, lamplight flashes behind a windowpane, and an intense silence returns, broken by the click and scrape of a latch being lifted. DogFellow feels his chest tighten. Beside him BearCreature stills his quivering chops, while Slope emits a faint squeak. the Master opens his front door and walks the length of his porch before taking the three steps that lead down to the beach. It is all done with the greatest solemnity. His booted feet – which the simpler beast people regard as an indissoluble part of his body – thump on every wooden board, and there is the jangle of the keys, which he keeps hooked to his belt. He does not smile, or scowl, or show anything in between. He only stares at them; and even in the still shaded air his eyes gather all to him. The narrowness in DogFellow's chest rises and captures his neck in a tight collar. A few moments pass and then –

'Who am I?' he asks, his words loud and hard.

'The Master –'

'The Master –'

'The M-Master . . .'

The replies pop off like ineffectual gunfire. DogFellow finds his tongue too sluggish as he stumbles over the phrase.

'What? What was that?' he says, his voice stern. 'I did not hear you. When I speak you must answer. Have you learned nothing? Have you forgotten since yesterday? I can't believe that. So: again. What am I?'

DogFellow and the others cry out in unison.

'And what must you do?'

'We must obey.'

'And what must you obey?'

'We must obey the Master's word.'

'And what is this word?'

'The word is the Law.'

'And what is the Law?'

'The Law is fivefold.'

'And what is the first of its parts?'

Thus begins the catechism, and the beast people call out – as they have been taught – that the Master is their maker, their father and mother, their protector and giver; that all beast people must live and work and do all they can to honour him; that all beast people are different but equal, and must live in peace and amity; that no beast person must drink save from a cup, or eat save from out of a bowl, and all foulness must be kept privy, and done according to the Master's instruction.

'And the fifth part of the Law? What does it tell us?'

'No one must go with another. No one must press his flesh against the flesh of another, for this is the most evil of things.'

'And what does the Master hate?'

'He hates this thing, this pressing of the flesh.'

'And why does he hate it?'

'For it is evil, the most evil of things, the pressing of the flesh.'

The Master stands before the line with his hands clenched behind his back; and as the reply echoes out across the beach, to disappear on the waves, he nods.

'Good. You did not forget, nor shall you. Obey the word of the Law. Obey, and you will please me.'

Three

They breakfast on mashed yam, collecting their plates to go and sit in the lee of the House of Food, for the sun is fast rising, and the shade keeps the flies off. They take it in turns to cook and serve, and the meals are always bland and often badly done, but no matter.

'Have you finished?' asks BlueBob, his goggling face inches from DogFellow's raised spoon.

'Does it look as if . . . ?' says DogFellow, taking a mouthful.

'You want that little bit there?' BlueBob wonders. His breakfast is a memory. He is as hungry as he was before he ate it.

'Mm-hmm,' says DogFellow, scooping up more while still chewing.

'Pff!' says BlueBob in disgust, but he loiters near, his compulsion to scrounge irresistible. For him, the scene is an unfolding tragedy.

'What you want food for anyhow?' he says, unable to bear it. 'You do not work, not properly.'

'Yes I do,' insists DogFellow, licking the corners of his mouth.

'Not properly, not lifting stones and carrying them. That's properly. Proper work! All the way – you walk a thousand steps sometimes. I counted. I know counting. A thousand steps all the way properly, like this –'

BlueBob, who has been busy building the jetty, swings his large rough hands down to his groin and cups them there, so that the sinews are drawn out along his fuzzy arms.

'– it is hard work. All the way from the forest to the sea, and watch where you drop it or your foot be crushed all to bits, like that pig chappie. He screamed: *Weeee!* No more work for him, true enough, but more for me. Hard hard work. And I say to you – what are you doing all this time?'

'I work,' says DogFellow, scraping his spoon across his plate and sucking on it.

'You? Pfff!'

BlueBob averts his face and begins to get up.

'You counting bottles all day long, and making marks with a dirty twig. I know. I have seen it. I laughed and said to the next beast, "Hey, look in there," and when he saw he laughed too.'

'You shouldn't have been spying. But to show I like those who carry the stones, here: I give you this.'

He thrusts the circle of polished tin into BlueBob's hand.

'Don't forget to take it in,' says DogFellow, and getting

up himself begins to walk away, back towards the Master's house.

The good humour of the previous moment evaporates as he draws near. The building squats, low and massive, its mix of basalt blocks and imported bricks producing a strangely mottled look, like a reptile's skin. He does not approach the outer door, with its palm-wood veranda and commanding prospect of the assembly field – that is sanctified earth, and forbidden to him. Instead he walks to the rear, passing through the gates of the palisade and crossing the enclosed yard. Instinctively, as he goes by the gatepost, he pauses, sniffs at it and senses a tremor in his right leg, which he stifles.

Unlike BlueBob, he has experienced no desire to count the number of steps he must take, but if ever he did, he would learn that twenty-three will carry him to the back door of the house. If, halfway across, he were to turn due right, another eighteen steps would deliver him to the door of the place he thinks of as the abode of misfortune – the hall of the sick – but which the Master calls the infirmary: whitewashed and wooden-slatted and staring malevolently at him. Turn left instead of right and he'd soon be amidst the cages, mercifully empty for now. But at this hour – at this appointed time – he is to tread a straight path, neither dawdling nor deviating, and his heart beats hard, for now he will be alone before *Him*, and those eyes will be fixed solely on his bowed head.

He can scarcely find the will to knock on the window. He can smell the Master's presence moments before the door is opened. The gruff voice orders him inside. As always he must halt and display the soles of his crooked feet, to show that they are clean, or at worst a little dusty, and won't besmirch the carpets that line the hall and the adjacent rooms. DogFellow knows he does not really belong in this part of the house, which is dignified by the name of East Wing. It is here that the dining room is, and the study too, and the private place to which the Master retires at ten every night. The chemical reek and the stink of cut flesh may still linger in the air, drawn down from elsewhere, yet polish and mothballs and the somnolence of the hour of breakfast, of lunch, of dinner (taken at eight, twelve and seven, without fail) are a potent counterweight.

Now, before the morning's lesson can begin, the Master stands there, talking out of the side of his mouth, his hands busy at the pipe he has clenched between his teeth, explaining how the instruments he will use that afternoon are to be sterilized, and in what manner they must be put in and out of the carbolic solution. Gazing down, DogFellow can see a vivid splash of blood like an elongated teardrop staining the cloth of the Master's trousers a little above the turn-up on the right leg. He pushes it out of his mind, and listens with nerve-racked intensity to what he is being told. He says 'Yes' and again 'Yes,' and then 'No' and then 'I will', while, with a drawn out *Mmmm* of satisfaction, the Master finally manages to light his plug of tobacco.

'But first,' he says, shaking the lit match to smoky

extinction, 'first you can come with me. It's important you practise your reading.'

DogFellow nods, thrilled and terrified, and in a daze he follows the Master through to the little room beside the parlour, with its school desk and old map on the wall showing the world in pink and green. He sits in a chair (and how strange that is!) with the thin book laid out flat before him. His hands shake, out of the mix of love and dread. The lesson begins.

'What about that?' asks the Master, moving around behind DogFellow's back.

'It is a 'C', Master,' says DogFellow.

'And what is C for?'

DogFellow has no need to seek for clues in the drawing of the burly quadruped with the bell about its neck.

'Cow,' he says.

'Good, very good. And the words listed underneath? Read them out to me.'

DogFellow does as he is told, forcing himself to be painstaking, deliberate, and to pause after each go for the Master's approving grunt, or else a tut and a brusque correction. In this manner DogFellow has been taken in hand, and taught to manage the alphabet, and read a few words, the better to assist and fetch and carry.

Yet it so happens that on this day the keen interrogation is anything but, and the good doctor, clumping about, is heard turning pages and humming to himself, only occasionally pausing to remark on the competence of Dog-Fellow's efforts. In between 'fox' and 'goose' there comes a flurry of muttering, and when – quite absorbed – he pauses to rest directly behind DogFellow's left shoulder, a new scent is suddenly released into the room, seeping off the squares of creased, closely written paper held between thumb and forefinger. Instinctively, Dog-Fellow sniffs the air and immediately dreads a clout from the hand that chastises. No blow follows, however, for the Master is sunk in what he's examining and talking under his breath, saying odd things which cannot quite be made out. DogFellow – whose ears are acute, but whose nose is non-pareil – sniffs again, and then again. It is the smell of strangers he is smelling, the smell of a strange male hand, a proper man's hand to be precise, exactly like the Master's own, and devoid of all suspicion of beast. And at that moment he is put to recalling how, the day before – or perhaps the day before that – a boat had put in, such as no one had ever seen or known before, only to quickly go away again – so quick, in fact, that most beast people doubted the evidence of their own senses. Was it *this* that had been brought – a few pieces of paper, carried across the wide Pacific?

DogFellow suspects he has unwittingly learned something secret, something forbidden, and tries to wish it away and continue with his pronunciation of 'I', which he stumbles over. The Master does not react, for he is enclosed within himself and quite oblivious. Then, as if waking up, he looks about and with a wave gets Dog-Fellow to close his text.

'I go now?' he asks.

'Yes. Go.'

DogFellow climbs down from the chair.

'No. Wait.'

The Master feels an irresistible need to speak.

'You must tell no one else, but there is to be someone new coming here, another Master, as it were. An American; a journalist. You understand?'

DogFellow looks wide-eyed, not understanding at all.

'I am to be written up, for a wide readership. I believe, in fact, for an international readership –'

He pauses, as if surprised to hear the fact spoken aloud.

'I confess,' he declares, 'at this late stage, to re-enter the fray . . .'

Like the prince in the play (a copy of which, bound in green Morocco, is rotting in a case not six feet away) he is suddenly stricken with doubt. It runs through him, like a pin through a butterfly. He quells it.

'But why not, why not, damn it all?'

He begins to pace up and down, in a fury of distraction, the keys on his belt rattling. It is as if, at that moment, he has finally convinced himself as to the necessity of this course, and having made up his mind he yields to the notion that at last he might have found the means of telling a world which thinks him dead – a spent force, a joke – that he survives and has discovered much.

'Of course, he must come. It is the first step. The first, and then . . .'

He stops pacing and stands in the middle of the room, arms folded, puffing in a frenzy on his pipe, already perceiving, through wreaths of smoke, the amanuensis at the table, receiving the gospel on how animals might become men.

DogFellow, his nose provoked, sneezes.

'Hmmph!' he says, the vision clearing. 'You still here? Go on, away with you. To your chores. Only remember – not a word.'

And he goes back to rereading his letter.

The rest of the night was awful. DogFellow returned to his bed, only to doze and wake and sleep again, a prey to sudden sweats and frights. At some point he thought he could hear them, whispering behind the sack he had for his front door.

'Hector!' he screamed. 'Fantine!'

He felt he could not move, that some dire trick had been played to make his arms and legs heavy, like logs, with another log rolled across his chest. It was just as it was in the infirmary, after he had fallen, after he had been chased, after all those things –

Sweating and panting, he somehow found the strength to throw his plate through the dark. It hit the far wall and dropped down with a clang.

'I see you!'

Yet he saw nothing – or not them, at least. He lay on his back and wished for the day, despite what it might bring. The darkness seemed unending and eventually he grew sure that he must have somehow fallen back to sleep, to pass witless through the sunlight hours, only to wake again as night returned. The thought created in him such anguish that he felt it was not one log which lay across his chest but a forest's worth: that he had in fact been buried beneath all the wood in the world and must lie immured in darkness, alive yet not alive, for ever.

At last, exhausted by all this thinking, he lost consciousness.

When he awoke it was light, with sunbeams poking in across the dirt floor, showing where the plate had fallen. He smacked his sticky mouth and sat up. At first he was dazed, and scrabbled about with the idea that he had missed roll-call. Then he realized when it was. As if to exorcise the ghost of times past he went to his door and pulled aside the sackcloth. The huts opposite were ruinous and deserted. No one moved about on the path. He stood there for a few distracted moments, but then a sudden impulse took him and he quickly went back in and rolled up his bedding, exposing the mattress of dried palm fronds and leaves. He reached into the middle, pushing his hand down into the crushed mass. Was it there? He recalled seeking it in the dark, or at least going through the motions. And what if they'd already been and robbed him, stealing away his most precious, his most secret possession? But no. Relieved, he felt his fingers brush against the square of newspaper. Very carefully, he pulled it out. He paused, listening: even his keen ears could locate no sound, other than the distant, desultory tweeter of island birds. He unfolded the scrap, holding it by the edges, which were rough and uneven, as if torn.

It was something he'd found long ago, wrapped about a bottle of sal ammoniac, for the Master's supplies of chemicals, like his supply of animals, came from else-where, from over the sea. DogFellow, set to the task of unpacking the wooden crates, would end up ankle-deep in straw and crumpled newsprint, too dense and black for him to make much sense of. And besides, what should he know of any world other than the one he lived in?

Yet the thing he had hold of now was of a different order. It did not tell of impossible things: it showed them. For the hundredth time – for the thousandth – he read the cartouche scrolled across the top of the page, mouthing the words with a slow and pleasurable exactness. It said:

A Scene from the Tuileries Gardens, Paris.

The picture below presented a sweep of trees and lawns, with buildings in the distance such as he had sometimes dreamed of, rising up like cliffs of unsullied whiteness. The people moved to and fro, on foot or seated in carriages, and the carriages were pulled along by the strange four-footed animals he knew went under the letter 'h'. H, which was for horses. Some people had their legs showing, others were half immersed in tiny bell jars: these, he realized, were the women. Those positioned far away appeared as specks, like fleas. Those nearer had their torsos and limbs etched out and walked by themselves or in twos and threes.

Above all, he was drawn to the figures who were closest, fitting just inside the frame of the picture. First was a man, strolling down the path, with trees on either side – not palm trees, or any of the other kinds found in the forest, but tall, graceful trees, bearing a full crown of tiny leaves. The man's features were grainy, although Dog-Fellow thought he could see the face, and would recognize it, if ever he needed to: a high forehead, a good nose, dark eyes and fine whiskers. The man wore a cravat and a frock coat. DogFellow coloured it a light grey and loved its beautiful cut, and the way it held itself to the crook of the man's arm. In his hand he carried a cane. On his head he had a tall hat. His feet were small, black and pointy. Across from him appeared two other people. They had similarly been subjected to the closest possible examination. One of them was another man, and although he had his back to DogFellow, the coat, the hat, even the cane were patently the same. The other was a woman, wearing a long trailing skirt, which meant her legs and her feet were invisible: perhaps she went unshod, although DogFellow considered this unlikely. What captured him more than anything was her face, for she had her head turned, showing her features in profile, and these were delicate and beautiful. Her hair was thick and lustrous and fell down over her shoulder in a gentle curve, such as might be drawn in damp sand. She had a hat of her own, so little it was hardly there. Nevertheless, if DogFellow looked close enough he could make out that there were feathers in it. They should be red, he thought; or red and blue intermixed. And finally, to complete the picture, there was a fourth person. He was taking the air himself, coming down the path towards the lady, and strolling with an ease and a lightness he had known only in the best of his dreams. Who was it? Who else could it be, with his elegant demeanour, and his back as straight as the cane he also carried? He saw her, and smiled shyly; he tilted his hat, and gave a slight inclination of the head. She, so beautiful and gracious, returned his silent greeting. She admired him, admired his bearing and his insouciance and his whiskers, which in their sleekness and lustre were as fine a set as she had ever beheld. Perhaps the two of them would stop and talk; or perhaps they will pass each other, on this summer evening in the Tuileries Gardens, Paris.

DogFellow's eyes grew misty with the pleasure and the consolation these thoughts brought him. He knew the word for it: a word he had learned, although he did not remember where; a difficult word, and a strange one, compounded of the sleekness of snakes and the buzzing of bees. A hard word, but wonderful and lovely all the same. He said it now, out loud.

He opened his mouth and said 'Civilization.'

Four

The American journalist Truman Henderson arrives with the next ship. The beast people don't know it, seeing only the snub-prowed steamer moored beyond the reef, and the toing and froing of the supply boat, its bow buried low in the surf by the weight of the cages it brings. They loiter beyond the beach, banished to the hem of the forest by the Master's stern order. Even DogFellow must keep hidden, though his fate entails being confined to the storeroom, where bottles are to be stacked and boxes unpacked. Through a small barred window high above his head and facing seaward he can hear the occasional shout and the sound of an unknown voice urging men – true men – to shift harder. A pained cry, altogether animal, sets Dog-Fellow's teeth on edge, and there is growling too. Then, growing louder, he recognizes the Master talking, only the usual harsh imperative tone has grown shaded and mellow. Offering a reply is a second speaker, whose voice is strange beyond reckoning.

'. . . I very much look forward to it –' he is saying, as

DogFellow, separated by a wall, cocks his head – 'your ideas are quite extraordinary.'

'It is a refreshing change to find such open-mindedness,' replies the doctor, and then adds something else, but already they have moved away, and DogFellow is left to stand and scowl, for the thought of a new Master perturbs him.

Some time later the old Master appears and says he must bide a while longer. Anxious, he does as he is told, sitting on an unopened wooden box full of lint and bandages. It begins to grow dark. The dinner hour comes and goes. Recently it is he who has learned to cook for the Master, preparing simple dishes on the stove that sits in its own nook, close by the place of cuts and stitches. Tonight, however, his duties are suspended. He listens. He can hear their babble. Once or twice he is able to snare a word, making it palpable on his own tongue, but for the most part the sound is closer to a rill of water, rushing over stones, or like the shifting colours of the sea.

More striking still are the smells that begin to creep in on the slightest of draughts – at first a dizzying mix of man odour, followed by the giddy whiff of roasted meat, and then, all at once, burning candles and tobacco smoke and alcohol. The last is a smell he detests, for it torments his nose when he sterilizes the Master's bloodied instruments. Yet this time the raw edge is bated by different elements, faintly fruity and peculiar. It scents the Master's breath when he finally tramps down the corridor and opens the door. His face, normally so graven, is as soft as butter. His cheeks, above the silver line of his beard, are red. In his hand he holds a hurricane lamp, illuminating DogFellow, who has waited in the dark with infinite patience.

'Come on; come with me,' he says, and DogFellow scrambles up, unable to contain the spontaneous joy he feels, his frets and apprehension forgotten.

They pass not to the left, which would take them to the rooms of work, where the bleached wooden trestles rest before shelves of bottles, but to the right, past the place where he learns his letters, then past the wall-mounted ship's barometer that has hitherto marked an absolute end to all that DogFellow knows. He is now walking down the passage which leads to the Master, who up ahead, treads heavily, even a little unsteadily. They pass a closed door, where the Master sleeps, and approach another that is half opened. The brief sound of purling liquid is heard from within, and the bell-like *ting* of glass striking glass.

'Wait,' he is told, and DogFellow feels the gentle pressure of a palm upon his crown. Trembling all over, he gratefully presses his back to the cool plaster while the Master steps forward to push the door fully open. He hears him say, 'I have something to show you that I think will be of considerable interest –'

There is an indecipherable reply and moments later, in a perfect daze, he stands before a table littered with the detritus of a large dinner. A silver candelabrum lights the room, which is very warm. In recognition of this the man who is seated, and who regards DogFellow with abject stupefaction, has already removed his tie and undone several of the buttons on his shirt. He attempts to put his freshly filled glass back beside his plate, but misjudges, and the glass topples on to the table cloth and spills its purple content over fork, plate and napkin. DogFellow is very alarmed and would shrink back into the shadows, but that irresistible hand is pressing him between the shoulder blades.

'Naturally,' the Master is saying, 'this is only a beginning. But it verifies everything I've addressed so far. You must agree, it's better than any quantity of theorizing.'

'His face –' says Henderson – 'what – what happened –?'

'Happened?' exclaims the doctor, a little indignant. 'Don't you understand? Go forward.'

The order is for DogFellow's benefit and he allows himself to be pushed until the table's edge is up against his chest.

'Turn your head this way. Now, turn it that way –'

The Master guides DogFellow, a finger pressed underneath his chin.

'– you can clearly see how I have amended the prognathous disposition of the skull, realigning it from a laterally compressed structure towards something far more open, where the cranial arch is dominant –'

All at once a full understanding of what he is being shown crashes in upon Henderson. Urged on, his trembling hands reach out to feel at the thin sutures which run like lines of longitude down DogFellow's arms, torso and legs. Here lies the proof of what was vaguely promised and hinted at in letters sent across the sea: the appalling marvel of manufactured flesh. A moist speck of chicken sits at the corner of Henderson's small mouth and DogFellow watches it as those same hands creep about the circuit of his skull, finding the presence of metal pins and plates beneath the patchily tufted scalp.

'Well, it beats everything I thought possible,' Henderson says, but he is checked with a little cluck, and insistently told that it is merely the fulfilment of ideas put forward two decades before.

'Unfortunately no one would give me leave to carry on my work, free from interference, and so I had to come here, which is in truth nowhere, and on my own, and without help of any kind, strive to put theory into practice . . .'

The Master's mood shifts, grows more terse.

'Quick,' he says to DogFellow, 'show him your hands.'

DogFellow obediently lifts them and lets Henderson look. The backs are heavily scarified, yet the regeneration of skin on the palms is such as to give a first impression of almost natural smoothness. Only the fingers disappoint, being stumpy, coarse and oddly mottled. Yet Henderson, squeezing the slightly pulpy flesh and feeling the bone beneath, is dry-mouthed with wonder.

'You took an animal paw . . .' he says, half rhetorically, and the Master, eager to expatiate, begins to run on the differences between plantigrade and digitigrade morphology, and the alignment of muscle and sinew.

'The thumb presented me with enormous difficulty,' he says, 'being entirely lost among canids. A monkey should have been far better, and yet my principles – my principles allowed for a reversion to the mammalian archetype, which has the digit placed exactly so, on an axis that can allow for eventual opposability; and so . . .'

His voice calm, his eyes glittering, the Master takes up the carving fork and with its prongs traces invisible arabesques all over DogFellow's palm, explaining each and every slice and how, over long weeks, the entire architecture of hand and wrist had been sculpted.

'Needless to say,' he adds, sweeping the fork up the arm and over DogFellow's face till it pricks at his forehead, 'there had to be a crucial reformation of the neural processes here as well; a thumb like that is entirely useless unless there is corresponding mental enhancement.'

'He really seems to understand you,' says Henderson.

'He could understand me when he had four legs. There's hardly any magic in it. I wanted something more. Isn't that so?'

He smiles at DogFellow, who has struggled to bound after the racing words which fill the room. He is also agonizingly aware of the chicken carcass on the table and the smears of chicken juice which mark his right palm and lie as twin dots upon his brow. Nevertheless, the realization that he is being addressed and that some order of reply is required proves powerful enough to break through the giddy circles of thought filling his head, and he says, 'Yes, Master.'

'My God, my God,' mutters Henderson, his hand rising to cup his mouth.

There is a whisper in DogFellow's ear: 'Tell the other Master what you were doing when I went to fetch you earlier.'

'I,' begins DogFellow, 'I was in the dark, waiting.'

'No, before then.'

'I put the bottles on the shelf and put all the boxes away.'

'So you see, he has his uses,' says the Master, but Henderson is not properly listening and repeats himself, saying 'My God' three or four times more. There is something ineffably disconcerting in the way DogFellow shifts his jaw: the action is without any fluency and proceeds rather through a rapid sequence of jerks, twisting violently left and right. This impression above all others bears down upon the man, though he is also struck by the quality of the voice, which is thin and flat and so strangely accented that even the simple story of the boxes required an absolute effort to make sense of it.

'Of course,' says the Master, returning to his explanations, 'these levels of attainment – particularly the primitive literacy skills he's developed – are hardly universal at present. I suppose I've made him a special project: dogs are so eminently malleable to begin with. Yet even my earliest and least successful ventures can manage some simple phrases: their ABCs, etcetera. It's principally a question of reshaping the tongue and the larynx . . .'

And he wants DogFellow to open his mouth and show the pink and white patchwork, but Henderson asks, 'How many are there, Doctor?'

'What?'

'How many of these – these people . . . ?'

'There were thirty-four. I've lost six or so.'

'Then you have twenty-eight others like . . .' Henderson, again overcome, can only point at DogFellow.

'Oh no, not at all. I've been bold in all my endeavours. And besides, I never could be sure as to which forms would yield the best, that is the most favourable results. This specimen here was patently derived from a dog. But I've worked with cats – big cats and a few middle-ranking sorts – bears, apes most obviously, – ah – a sloth, pigs, goats . . .'

The Master talks clearly and keeps nothing from Henderson, who periodically shakes his head in astonishment. The indissoluble bonds between physiology and the chemical rhythms of life are carefully expounded, and the possibilities inherent in surgical intervention explained.

'I confess that the exact processes whereby the animal brain is capable of reformulation, until it takes on something approaching the complexity of the human mind, is only partially clear to me. I know only which procedures will achieve the desired results. Yet I'd venture that what we consider intelligence is less a product of brain mass than of connectivity. It may well be that our own grey matter, which we esteem so greatly, is gross in its quantity – hardly so much is needed to think and to function. It is mere packing, to fill out our heads and provide the circumference needed to properly wear a hat.'

Henderson is too much in awe to laugh at this unexpected jest, or even to make a reply. The Master, worked on by the pleasure of hearing his own exposition, as well as by the amount he's drunk, does not take offence and continues talking, halting only to dab at his damp and florid face with a napkin.

'Quite patently, we see how all life is a continuum, Mr Henderson. We may believe that our high foreheads and verbal genius make us a different order of beast – which is to say no beast at all – yet that is merely to let the old religio-spiritual mumbo-jumbo into our scientific pantheon. The very fact that I can take you to a cat that is capable of some very moderate reasoning, and that can count up to ten, ought to make the world realize that brains are nothing special. Getting him over there to walk on his hind legs: *that* was more of a feat of the surgeon's art.'

He indicates towards DogFellow. Henderson is wide-eyed. When he goes to take his recharged glass there is a slight tremor in his hand.

'And are there – are there any limitations you would recognize, Doctor?' he asks.

'Certain laws of physics I suppose – perhaps others . . .'

'I feel I ought to be writing this down,' Henderson mutters, and even casts his hand up to his breast pocket, as if looking to take out his fountain pen.

'Later, later,' he is told. 'We'll have time enough for all that. I'll explain what the world ought to know.'

But not before DogFellow, whose head is in a dreadful spin, gets sent, shuffle-footed, to bed.

It was the evening of the next day and DogFellow, stooping low, studied the earth and the tracks that four feet, falling in tandem, had left. They had walked by here very recently, he was sure of it. He stared hard, to make sure, but the strain made him blink. In that fading light, on the trampled ground, there were puddles of black and grey intermixed, sliding over one another like spectral slugs or amoebae. His poor eyes! He rubbed at them; they ached and performed tricks, conjuring points of light and sooty prickles. Yet he knew Hector and Fantine came this way. Their scent lay like a long thin cloud along the winding path, and he thought he could catch the distant susurration of voices, distinct from the sound of the leaves or the evening breeze. DogFellow was not graceful – how could he be, with those crooked legs? – but, true to that brutish portion of his name, he was dogged, and he set out to chase the trail of those malefactors – those criminals – those breakers of the Law. The going was hard all the same. On this part of the island, on the eastern flank, no

44

one ever went, or had ever gone, apart – apart from old Fiddler.

Oh!

DogFellow hated to suddenly think the thought. It was like a big spiderweb sprung in his face. He wiped it away quickly, as he would the sticky threads, and pressed on, weaving about the buttresses of high trees, by secondary growth and fallen boughs, despite the ache and the rising sweat. Then, up ahead, as crisply and clearly as if his own ear was the cup intended to receive such purling words, he heard Fantine's voice . . .

'No, not here, you will get wet feet!'

. . . and DogFellow experienced the most peculiar mix of desire and yearning, running like a countercurrent against his other thoughts. He might, with the slightest acceleration (which even he could manage) catch up with them: they were dawdling, their destination vague, their appetites already sated, perhaps. But he had rehearsed the moment so minutely, spent such a time blowing on the hot coal of righteousness, that the prospect of actually living it out was too excruciating to bear. They were very near. He could hear the in and out of Hector's panting and catch the pitter-pat of Fantine's small naked feet, as she stepped backwards out of the clearing.

'Catch me!'

. . . she called it out, and with a gruff woof Hector was in pursuit, the two of them going up over the ridge that would lead them north-westwards.

After a few moments more DogFellow resumed the trail, forcing his weary eyes, his weary mind, to register the way long-settled leaf mould had been scuffed over, or a twig snapped in half; yet it was his nose that truly guided him, as if he were an eel swimming in the ocean depths, and he snuffled up their commingled odours, going after the vapour trail that curled through the darkening forest. He slowed his pace and deliberately allowed the occasional sound of a voice to fade altogether.

The way grew steeper – a dislodged rock might go tumbling all the way down to the strand – and then DogFellow was walking down a cleft in the hillside, passing into a dusky gully, where the basalt innards of the island poked through its skin. Thick moss grew there, and ferns and other plants with high-arching stems and leathery, slatted leaves. At the very bottom flowed a stream, invisible beneath a concourse of shag-headed reeds. DogFellow stopped and impulsively stooped to gather a little puddle of water on his palm. It tasted very cold and gave him a brief sense of wellbeing – sufficient to let him conceive of giving up his futile chase and yield to the whimsical desire of rolling over and over in the damp, odoriferous and spongy carpet that he stood on. But he knew this place, or somewhere very like it. The thoughts which had startled him earlier returned, and this time he must go where they took him, far away into the past, to a time before Fantine, before Hector, and before even the time of the two Masters.

Ah, how he could remember –

Five

For once, when it begins, DogFellow does not see it. He is at his chores, in the yard squared off by its high fence. He has been given a hammer, which is heavy to hold, and he needs to use both hands. The purpose is to break up wooden boxes, drawing out the nails with the hammer's claw: a task as difficult as it is tiring. DogFellow, exasperated, grunts with vexation. The nail he is struggling to extricate buckles; the hammer slips and narrowly misses his shin. He plunders his tiny repertoire of cuss words and wishes the job was done. It is then – as he thinks this – that the cry goes up: a slovenly babble, spilt from some mouth, some patched tongue, followed by a shrill yell of pain. DogFellow's hair prickles. He lets the box fall on to its side. Behind him, in the place with the dusty shutters, there is a faint metallic clatter. The yell comes again, louder this time, and does not cease but rises and falls, each fall terminating in a double sob before breaking out once more.

'What is that noise? What is that noise!' exclaims the

Master, disturbed at his work table and now striding out, like angry Zeus descending from Olympus, not bothering to cloak his elemental self.

'You! What's going on?'

DogFellow, poor mortal, almost withers on the spot, blasted to the toe bones by this intemperate vision: jacket off, shirtsleeves rolled, crimson to the elbows and bearing the bloody knife.

'What is this noise!'

The palisade's great gate is unbolted; he casts it open with a bang.

'I order you to shut up!' he shouts, and disappears. The yelling dies back, but not altogether. DogFellow is filled with the compulsion to run about in a wild and useless circle. A sound he fears and dreads swells up in the base of his throat, making his head vibrate. He has dropped the hammer and now stands with his shoulders sloped forward, his entire body as taut as a bowstring. Outside, the noises – the angry shouting of the Master; the sickening cries of the other – have ceased. Long moments pass and then, with a grunt of effort, the Master reappears. Over his shoulder and around his neck there is the thin hairy arm of a beast person. DogFellow, beside himself, scuttles forward and lets out a volley of barks.

'Shut up, you imbecile,' says the Master. 'Quickly, help me.'

He tilts to the right, allowing the sagging body he has been carrying to subside beneath its own weight. Through the fog of terror and excitement DogFellow sees that it is Jackdaw, one of the ape-men, one of those he is a little frightened of and secretly despises. Now, too late and too timid, he lets him collapse in the dust.

'You useless –' exclaims the Master, although in truth he himself is half distracted with the shock of it: bursting out on to the hot, hard-baked parade ground only to see one of his progeny savaging another, contemptuous of the most sacred precept, the most inviolable law –

There is blood, spreading now in the dirt by Dog-Fellow's feet. The Master heaves Jackdaw on to his back, exposing the gouges raked in parallel lines across the ribcage and about the belly. The canvas trousers that Jackdaw wears are turning black about the crotch, and he shudders, his mouth parting to show the bulge of his tongue jammed between his teeth. The eyes are open but display white only. DogFellow sees the way the throat is awash with red bubbles, the wind whistling through a jagged, meaty rip.

'Stay there,' orders the Master and runs into the house. DogFellow surrenders to a low whimper. He bows down, almost about to take Jackdaw's big, man-size hand, but then thinking better of it; and here is the Master back again, carrying one of his silver dishes. All he says to DogFellow is 'Get out of my light!' before setting to work with needle and thread. He stitches at great speed and with unerring accuracy. Jackdaw, half-conscious, begins to sob and tremble. When he has done, the Master looks about and then tuts in annoyance. Bending very low, as if to kiss the body, he snips the thread with his teeth.

'Now I need you,' he says to DogFellow, and together they succeed – though not without several rebukes that

drop on DogFellow's head – in half lifting and half carrying Jackdaw across the yard into the dusty shade of the
empty infirmary, with its odours of sickness and lamp oil
and pain. They lay him on a raised pallet, across which a
coarse sheet has been spread. The Master chafes the skin
on the soft underpart of Jackdaw's wrist and presses a
needle into his vein, expertly injecting him. Afterwards he
waits a while, watching as the hapless man-beast subsides
into settled unconsciousness. It is only as he re-crosses the
yard, tailed by DogFellow, that the questions begin.

'What do you know of this?'

'Master?'

'This – this! Don't play the fool with me!' His anger is
suddenly magnificent. 'It was one of your so-called
brothers who did it!'

DogFellow, quaking, says 'I – I –' and that is all he says,
before the words glue to his dry tongue.

'I saw him. It was Fiddler. He ran off. Of course he
would, the filthy creature. Have they quarrelled before?'

'No, Master.'

'Look at me when I'm talking to you!'

They pause on the steps, about to go back into the
house. DogFellow peers abjectly up into the face of his
angry god. There are tiny flecks of blood in God's white
beard. DogFellow fears he is about to piss himself, as Jackdaw has done.

'Did something happen between those two? Something
that you haven't told me about?'

'No, Master,' repeats DogFellow, who would never lie,
knowing how those eyes, that once looked under the hard

dome of his pate and into the coralline swirls of his brain, thus gained the power to do the same forever after.

'No, Master, no. Never.'

Indeed, DogFellow is bewildered to consider that old Fiddler, possessed of only three teeth and with his hair all eaten up by time, could ever have mauled a beast person as brawny and fierce as Jackdaw.

'Well, I'll get to the bottom of it,' snaps the Master. 'You are supposed to love one another. Love one another!'

He suddenly bawls this at poor, overwrought Dog-Fellow, who quails accordingly.

'What is the purpose of the Law when this can happen! What is the point? It ruins everything, can't you see that? Christ, I ought to kill the lot of you! Wipe you all from the face of the earth, you miserable vermin. That's right: vermin!'

If, at that moment, DogFellow could coil in on himself, coiling and coiling until he was nothing but a compact, insensate and heedless ball, then he would. Yet he must bear witness, as the Master, incandescent with wrath, storms down to his workplace, swinging his jangling keys. DogFellow cannot help himself; he must follow, no matter what, until suddenly ordered to *stay*.

He listens as doors suddenly slam, drawers slide in and out and an unvarying barrage of denunciation is blown into the overheated air.

'Kill,' the Master says repeatedly, 'kill – you – all. Every last one of you. Cockroaches! Treat me like this. Bite my hand. Behave that way, well, I'll show you, you'll learn one final lesson –'

DogFellow's delicate ears catch every mortifying syllable, buffeted amidst the thud and grind of things being shoved about. He knows the pitch at which each door swings open and can tell the difference between the locks on the tall glass cupboards: the one that yields with a sudden click; the one that puts him in mind of sand grains held between gritted teeth, the one that jams. But the dull pop he now discerns belongs to none of these; the creak that follows he doesn't know either. Something heavy hits against solid wood, then for a few moments there is silence. What is happening? Is the Master going to go away forever and leave him there? Past caring he starts to whine, until the bang-bang of returning feet excites a fresh surge of fear, gratitude, adoration. He will swoon, he is sure of it: if there are to be killings, then let him expire now, yielding himself in an excess of boot-licking – let him do that, and choke out his life and his love.

'Now then –'

The Master is in the doorway, a black staff held under one marmoreal arm. But, sniffs DogFellow, it is not a staff, for it carries an odour of metal and some strange oil he can't recognize.

'– where did I put the cartridges? Don't just stand there staring! Come in here and look under that table, in the box marked for clamps. It's a brown paper container I'm after, around about eight by eight –'

He breaks his staff in half, though the two halves do not come away. There is something connecting them, like with scissors. Then he is up the other end of the room, foraging with one hand behind tight rows of jars.

'Damn it!' he exclaims, as he gets a splinter from the roughly finished shelf. He turns about and glares at DogFellow.

'What did I just say to you? Come on! Go and look – a box, eight by eight, plain brown paper sealed with wax. What's the matter? Don't you understand English any more? Has this whole place gone completely mad?'

Mouthing some reply – though the words have lost all cohesion – DogFellow stumbles over to where he is directed, yet, before he lays a hand to help, the Master growls significantly and is pulling at the flaps of his prize. It is such a box as could contain any small thing – he has dozens stowed away – but what he shakes out looks altogether different from the usual run of surgical blades, bandages and chemical compounds. Two cylinders, thumb-length, dull card for the upper body and then glittering brass. One after the other they are slotted into the staff's broken gullet. Next, with a snap, the breach is repaired.

'That's it . . .'

Raising his arm, stretching out his other hand to support the weight, the Master lines up the muzzle with DogFellow's face.

'Don't move,' he says. DogFellow does not move.

'A sovereign remedy,' he mutters.

'M-master?'

DogFellow sees how he is being squinted at, down the length of the barrels.

'If you all had only one head I swear I'd blow the bloody thing off and have done with it. Then, to start again. To begin from scratch. And to get it right the next time. There's enough divine precedents.'

He talks out of the corner of his mouth.

'Oh yes. A very tempting proposition,' he says, but he suddenly seems tired of the thought and straightens up, lowering the gun.

'Come on. Take the leather pouch you use and put all the cartridges in it. We're going out.'

'Where, Master?' asks DogFellow.

'Hunting.'

Six

And back in the future DogFellow felt again the sensations that poured with the richness of arterial blood through his anxiety-racked, joy-racked body, as – the Master's gun hound for an afternoon – he sweeps up the cartridges and scampers after, out on to the porch.

The Master has already begun to strike at the great iron triangle that hangs by a yard of ship's hawser from a whitewashed wooden rafter. He hits the triangle with a short iron bar, to which it is chained, and the afternoon throbs with noise. DogFellow is still very frightened, yet something else now bids for dominance in the hub of his being: a new sensation that gains control over his pounding heart and makes him hop from one foot to another. For the second time that day the ghost of a bark is gathering in the back of his throat. His breath rises in fast, scalding pants.

Terrified by the clang-clang-clang, the beast people come shambling out from the shadow of the trees, or up from the sweet potato patches, or else can be seen lolloping along the line of the beach, their bodies hunched, their heads darting from side to side, as if in anticipation of some imminent terror. Row by row they form up and still the Master hammers away with his tireless arm. Dog-Fellow, uniquely, is not with his addled brethren but looks down on them. He sees how a few dare to glance to their neighbour, mouthing their incredulity –

'Look at DogFellow!'

'See how he stands, at the Master's hand!'

'What is it he knows?'

'How mighty he has grown!'

And DogFellow's heart swells, and he pulls the pouch he's shouldered around to cover his belly, so they can all see it and be amazed by this new mark of favour.

But quiet: the Master has ceased to belabour the iron triangle. He begins to speak in a voice that is appalled and appalling.

'A terrible thing has happened,' he says. 'A most terrible thing. I myself, your Father, your Maker, can scarcely begin to find the words to express it . . .'

None dare cast a sideways glance now. All eyes are focused on barely shuffling feet. One or two simple souls mutter aloud, but they are hissed to silence. The Master, on his platform, folds both arms across his chest and scowls mightily.

'You know the Law. You know the words of the Law, and what it is that I ask. More than anything I desire for you to live in peace and friendship: brother and brother, sister and sister. You and you and you –'

He has ceased to hold his arms folded and, with his

terrible hand extended, he picks off the beasts one by one. None, of course, will look – none will risk the thunder flash and the certitude of annihilation – though each in turn feels the weight of the Master's finger, as massive as the earth below, shadow their brow.

'Why must it be that a certain beast person chooses to cast my word down into the dust and trample on it? What evil thoughts could summon so wicked a thing? Do you know?'

There is an audible mumble: muted cries of astonishment and self-exoneration. DogFellow, consumed by his love for the power of the Master, shares in his disgust.

'And it happened here, in this place, an hour since. Blood, you wretched children – blood was spilt.'

To the mantra of exhalations conveying guiltlessness are added soft cries of 'No! No!'

'But yes. The one you know as Jackdaw lies near to death, his flesh torn, his pain terrible. Why? Why is this so? Because one of your own kind, your own brothers, set his teeth against him, biting and tearing, taking pleasure in these forbidden things and setting the Law you live by at nothing. Answer me: what shall be done with any beast person who breaks the Law?'

To this there is only a frightened silence.

'Shall this hand, that gave life, be withdrawn?'

The Master no longer points. His right hand is held palm outermost, paraded like a sacred relic before the faithful.

'It shall. It must. And what will take its place?'

DogFellow, entranced, sees what will follow inside his head before the act is played out.

'This. This, you benighted children.'

And it is the left hand, the hand that smites, which is displayed in a steady arc, back and forth.

'The one you call Fiddler: he has angered me. He has outraged you. He must be punished. Where is he now? I cannot see him among your number. He has run away, because he understands the punishment that is due to him for his wicked act. Run as fast as you can, Fiddler – that is what I say. Run, run. I, your Master, your Maker, pronounce sentence. I say that he who breaks the Law must himself be broken, smashed and destroyed, to the last bone in his body. And I will see it done this day, before the sun goes down.'

He has finished speaking. The rage that had possessed him has been sublimated into a frightening calm. Everything now is deliberate and measured. He turns and picks up the shotgun he has brought out of the house. For a moment he glances at DogFellow, whose heart thuds with joyous expectation, even while he simultaneously wishes to piss, to vomit, to discharge his bowels.

The Master lifts the gun up, assuming the firing position. The beasts look on, as amazed and uncomprehending as DogFellow was minutes before at the sight of this large, ugly and unwieldy stick. He shifts the stock against his right shoulder and picks out a vacant target above the heads of his doltish congregation. They wait. DogFellow waits. the Master, counting slowly and silently, reaches ten and says it aloud, and then –

They are on their backs, all of them, eyes wide with terror, paralysed by the sheer volume of noise that briefly breaks the still afternoon apart. The sound – an eructation, it seems, in the old volcanic heart of the island – echoes and re-echoes to the scream of whirling birds, whose black wings pass in front of DogFellow's eyes, though his eyes are tight shut. A pungent cloud turns about and about, hiding the Master entirely, until one smoky thread snags on the breeze and the cloud unravels, showing him to those that dare to raise their heads. He laughs and says, 'Stand up, the lot of you! Did I tell you to lie down?'

DogFellow, feeling his legs have gone, still contrives to get to his feet. All the other beast folk do the same.

'Now you may understand what awaits those of you who break the law,' says the Master. 'It is their fate to perish by my thunder.'

'It is their fate to perish by his thunder,' repeated Dog-Fellow, and the words were still strong enough to hammer like mallet strokes against his bones, as he left off remembering the fate of old Fiddler and thought once again of Fantine and Hector, who had passed that way minutes before, with the heat of the worst of things rising off them. But DogFellow, amidst the moss and the ferns, felt the coolness begin to cleave to him, while high above the red was fading away, and soon the stars would show themselves. He regretted his lapse into old thoughts, bad thoughts, and he started up a trot, further down the spongy gullet of rock, listening to the moist bumping of his footfall and the swish-swish of the reeds. Ahead, the trickle of the stream grew amplified and then faded away in a high-pitched splashing; the ground rose up and then suddenly disappeared – the rock had been cut clean away, leaving a sixty-foot drop that ran in both directions, north and south. DogFellow was not dismayed. He knew of it. He'd been there before –

Seven

'Faster! Stop slacking!'

The Master has paused somewhere up ahead, in between the barrel trunks of cycads. Climbing as fast as he can, DogFellow struggles to keep his tongue penned inside his mouth. A thin lick of sweat – all that the man in him can muster – lies between his hairy shoulders. The strap on the pouch of cartridges has begun to rub against his skin, through the coarse buff cloth of his shirt, which he has unbuttoned to below the bulge of his sternum. On DogFellow's right and left are other beast people, though he cannot see them. They form a chain, trawling up the island, all primed to screech if the renegade Fiddler should be sniffed or spotted. It is the Master's master plan. He spent half an hour of precious daylight explaining it, point by point, and has so ordered the hunt that everyone has his or her allotted place, with the dimmest and most docile appropriately assigned secondary roles to the rear of the advancing line. The Master himself was to have roved between the vanguard and the rest, his gun cocked, yet he is so impatient to exterminate the delinquent that he keeps running ahead and berating those whose appetite for vengeance is plainly wanting. Wherever the Master goes DogFellow must of course follow, though he is not quick, like Hector, or strong, like BearCreature. The going is especially difficult as, for the fifth or sixth time, the Master scolds all those who toil in his wake. He stands breathing lightly, watching DogFellow limp up to him.

'What's the matter with you?'

'Nothing. No matter —'

'Give me an extra pair of cartridges.'

While DogFellow fumbles, the Master unbuttons his breast pocket. He glances right and left.

'Go forward! Go forward! Don't stop because I have! Keep going forward!'

There is a heavy crash, as one of the bigger beasts kicks aside a fallen log. The cry 'Go forward!' – variously maimed by mouths unused to words of command – sounds faintly in either direction. DogFellow catches hold of the cartridges and offers them up.

'Just a minute,' says the Master.

He pulls a silver flask from inside his jacket and, pulling out the cork, takes a nip. He sniffs in a great lungful of air.

'We'll have him soon enough,' he says, and adds, 'I'll drink to that,' before taking a second swig. DogFellow remains with his arm outstretched, the very model of supplication.

'We'll catch the dirty runt, won't we, boy?'

The Master, exhilarated by the thrill of the chase, by the glow of the brandy, gives a benevolent smile and, as he takes the cartridges, runs his other hand over the top of DogFellow's head, roughing the patches of close-cropped hair. It is heedlessly done, casually accomplished, and DogFellow is overcome by such a sudden surge of joy that his eyes grow damp and his nose prickles. He imagines himself, as he has done in a thousand daydreams, saying, 'I love you, Master,' because he knows that word, *love*, realizes that it is congruent with the heady flux which swirls around his head and chest and heart; and indeed, in his dreams, it is always said at such a moment as this, with the two of them caught in some perilous endeavour, or else in the aftermath of danger, from which DogFellow has rescued his lord, sustaining perhaps that mortal blow that will let him die in the embrace of those strong white arms. These thoughts belong with his most secret secrets, nurtured in silence and fed in part by illicit, semi-literate study of the old scraps of newspaper that he sometimes finds in with the straw which cushions the Master's bottled powders. His eyes grow damper still. The feelings he has are too much. He will say it. He will tell him – '*I love you*' – but his voice is no more than a whisper, and the Master is already away out of sight. DogFellow readjusts his shoulder strap and follows.

By now it is late afternoon and the light runs like gold between the shadows of the forest. They are on a high place, and away to the west, where the sun sits, lies the great Pacific, foaming against the reef which encircles the island. The cycads have given way to tall trees with slender, naked trunks. The ground underfoot is patched with shrubs and is faintly damp and black.

'He is a good runner, hey, DogFellow?' says Handy, who has paused to sniff the air and scratch himself.

'Move on,' mutters DogFellow.

'Who would think it, with his old legs and old feet, that old one . . .'

Inflamed by the desire to serve, to die if need be, DogFellow is pricked by such talk.

'Don't speak well of that dirty runt. He has broken our law –'

'I hear you. I say only that if he must go lie under the earth then Jackdaw should go also. He was always bad talking against old Fiddler, and hitting him. You know it, DogFellow.'

But DogFellow does not listen, leaving Handy to loiter on for a few moments more while he follows the Master. A butterfly, bluer than the ocean, with vivid black eyes painted on its wings, flutters past his face. He waves it off. To the right, twenty paces away, there are two beast people strolling loosely apart, one of them swinging a stick, the other intent on studying the play of light and shade against tree bark. Behind him he can still hear Handy, talking to no one. He does not know where the Master has gone. Perplexed, he stops again and half consciously sniffs at the odour carried on the light breeze: a mineral smell, sufficient to pluck at the doggish chords that run right through him. He turns around and as he turns he is startled to see BlueBob four or five yards distant, peering at him through the gap in a small grove. He peers back, a little alarmed now, and instantly apprehends it is not himself who is the object of BlueBob's narrow-eyed stare; rather, it is the seeming bundle of sticks and rags that has contrived to wedge itself up among the boughs. One of the sticks moves stiffly and makes a forlorn gesture. DogFellow feels the breath leave him in a sudden wheeze. He moves left and right, tripping between possible actions. He sees that at last BlueBob has recognized him. They both continue to stare as the pitiful creature – the point on which they have all been converging – clings to its perch.

Why this hesitation? DogFellow is in a sudden rage at the paralysis which has settled hold of BlueBob. Why doesn't he cry out, hollering for the Master? But BlueBob does nothing save look, watching as Fiddler clings hopelessly, helplessly, to his tree. It is possible to make out the head, and half a face, pressed tightly to the bark. His clothes – so old and worn and patched – now lie in rags. The body beneath looks pallid and faintly leprous. One bleeding foot hangs down on DogFellow's side. Whatever the tsunami of fear that swept him so far and so high into the interior of the island, it is now spent, and he lies wrecked in a fork of the branches. And yet, conscious of these others, he struggles to raise himself up. At first it seems as if he is tumbling backwards, his ghost set free from its prison house. Then, with a scrabbling motion, he turns his fall into a drop, feet first. He lands awkwardly, with a pained *ooff!* He hasn't got the strength to run any more, or the will to plead, or even the capacity to acknowledge the half-dozen beast people who now watch him as he passes to the left, drawn by the sun, impelled by fear of the Master.

The Master! Suddenly he is there, ahead of them all, stepping out from behind the trees, buttoning his fly. Before he can react, DogFellow is crying out at the top of his voice and bounding forward to swipe at Fiddler. They go down in a tangle, rolling over once, twice.

'Get clear!' shouts the Master. 'Get away from him!'

DogFellow, his teeth bared, his hackles raised, stares furiously into Fiddler's upturned face, which is as thin and fragile as wet paper. Old Fiddler blinks back.

'It's you,' he says, vaguely startled.

A tremble runs through DogFellow's top lip.

'Step away,' he is told. DogFellow obeys. Fiddler can still see the sky through a fretted dome of twigs and leaves. Then the Master is there, standing over him, his shotgun pointing.

'See this,' says the Master to the beast people, who hang back, clinging to the shadows of the trees, 'this is the one who I said would pay the penalty. We have hunted him down, like the animal he is. I want you to watch me now. Are you watching?'

There is no noise from behind him. He could be alone on the island, with Fiddler at his feet. Irritated, he glances at DogFellow.

'You – are you watching?'

'Yes, Master,' says DogFellow.

But he closes his eyes the moment before the Master pulls the trigger.

Now he stood there, near the place where they'd thrown the criminal. The Master had spared DogFellow that duty, for DogFellow was always among the least robust of the beast people. Yet was any real effort required in scooping up Old Fiddler's torn and bloody remains? Up he'd come, borne by three sets of strong arms. The rag-like limbs swung once, twice, and then disappeared over the lip of rock, the body falling sixty feet, to be further smashed and pulverized. They had gathered, all of them, and peered down, just as a long time later DogFellow, alone, peered into the shadows that turned the drop into a tarn, full of coal-black water. He knew that Fiddler was still down there, immersed beneath leaf mould and the residues of time, his ancient yellow bones picked bare and lying in a tangled mound – long bones, short bones, ribs and back-bone, but no skull, no, for the head was gone.

DogFellow shivered to picture such a sight, and saw in quick succession other terrible things that he had borne witness to, that he had been responsible for, and it seemed *as if he himself was ready to fall forward, ready to be swallowed whole, as the black waters swirled and dilated. But even as the shadows ascended he could feel those strong hands at the scruff of his neck, lifting him clear, cupping his old stitched face and pinching his cheek. If he must remember, remember this: that the Master gave his creatures laws to live by, and those who breach the Law are no longer his, are no longer anything – no, not anything.*

DogFellow raised himself up, kindling his anger, his suspicions. He began to walk as fast as he was able, skirting the cliff, travelling back southwards. Hector and Fantine had deliberately walked in a loop, making a detour to the north because they thought no other would ever venture there. They did it out of fear and out of guilt; DogFellow was sure of it, but he was wise to their tricks, their devilment.

The air was grey, with the sun gone and only a diaphanous shred of moon to compensate. He walked for a long while, close to the edge of the sudden, rocky drop. Once he accidentally kicked a lump of basalt, which fell with several loud clunks as it struck the slope, but then the quiet returned. DogFellow knew that at last the high ground itself would begin to diminish, spreading out into the island's southern side, and he knew that those two had walked this way a while before. It was not scent or sight that told him this; it was something else, as taut as a string running through his body, which vibrated with each motion of the breeze and the growing hiss of the sea. He stopped at last, the ground beneath his feet now no more than a low undulation, rolling down to where earth and sand were intermingled. The forest behind him was silent. Ahead he could see the black clump of a coconut grove, and then the dusty flats that lay prostrate before the whoosh of the Pacific. He reached down and picked up a fistful of earth, crushing it against his nose. Part of him yielded at once to the splendours of this draught, with its multitudinous top notes, middle registers and undercurrents, carrying him this way and that: the odours of sweet decay, of salt, mineral stinks, fungus, faeces, water, resins and acids, redolent between each grain of dirt. He cast it down, half ashamed, and resumed his survey of the murky beach.

Were they there? He could hear no noise, except that which should exist – the eternal sounds. He could see nothing either. He considered again the iniquity of their transgression. True to say, he had watched birds pair together, snakes too, and for a few days each year the beaches became drenched with little silver fishes, dying on beds of their own seed. Yet these were creatures which did not issue from the Master's own hand, or if they did – DogFellow's theology was vague on this point – never enjoyed any special favour, merely being cast into existence, like the rocks or the stars, to live senselessly and without purpose. Thinking thus (as DogFellow did) the logic of the Master's universe became apparent: to those things that did not gather to adore him, the perpetration of the worst of things attracted no opprobrium. They had no law, no knowledge. How could they be cursed and punished? But for the beast people to so violate themselves . . .

He started forward again, though carefully, trying to see through the dark. Soon he was walking on hard com-

pacted sand and stepping between old coconut gourds and the yellow thatch of dead palm leaves. He set one hand on a tree trunk and looked up and down the beach. The place was ghostly, silent. The scrap of moon had gained in substance, and it yielded enough light to make the wet sand faintly luminous, while the surf seemed an endlessly recurring bar of dirty white. He could not be sure if the tide was coming in or going out.

After a few moments he quit the darkness of the palms and ventured out into the open. The beach grew cool and damp against the soles of his feet. He felt the urge to let the froth of the sea tickle his toes. The breeze had dropped. There was no odour in the air other than the everlasting odours of the island and the scent of the immense toiling ocean. Ahead of him, where the tracks led, there were no loitering figures, pale in the light of the meagre moon. They must have gone to the north once more.

Let them go, thought DogFellow. He had discovered all he needed of their disgusting perfidy. If there must be an actual witness to the grinding of flesh on flesh, then Lemura would speak out.

Resolved, DogFellow stood up and for the first time actually considered where he was and how he was to get home. When he thought on it, he was sure he was never out at such an hour before, whatever the hour might be, save perhaps once . . .

In truth, he had himself transgressed – the Master's word forbade any beast person to go beyond the perimeter of the huts after dusk. Yet if he transgressed, it was to hunt down a greater transgression – the greatest of all.

The Master would understand; indeed, when the Master returned all might be laid plain and bare, and everyone receive what was due to them, in full and furious measure. This idea excited DogFellow and he turned in a circle and threw back his head, ready to yip at the sky, as if the Master should appear there.

On the beach he closed his eyes. He felt the sand beneath his feet, carrying him away, into the past. It seemed a night fated for remembering . . .

Eight

'Hold steady.'

He keeps a tight grip on the kidney dish, into which shreds of blood-blackened thread fall.

'Come nearer.'

He does as he is told, shuffling on his bare feet, making patterns in the blood-speckled sand. He draws comfort from the gritty feel against his soles, and comfort too from this silent attendance in the shaded quiet of the house. He holds it to himself, warding off the creeping unease he senses elsewhere, in the corridors, out in the yard, in the dining room. Words have been traded. He does not grasp the exact meaning, but he understands the way emotion flows, running like a sea current. Henderson left the compound; he left the compound and went out on to the beach, terrifying those beasts at work on the jetty. They ran off, and the Master came out, very angry.

'Closer.'

He shuffles sideways like a crab, watching as the long labial scar that bisects the creature on the table is picked bare. It is – was – a cat, the puma, carried ashore with the American, sixteen days before. Now it appears something else altogether. First it had been tied and gagged and shaved: by this act alone the Master had revealed his power, to turn a predatory animal into something already half out of nature. Then, assisted by DogFellow, the pallid body had been washed down with warm water and soap, and wiped over with ether, before the Master (having put down his pearl-handled razor and taken up a fine brush) marked out his intended route using gentian violet. Only then might the proper work begin: cut, graft, resection, stitch, each action performed over long hours, by daylight and by lamplight. It is hard work, and secret too. The Master who is not a Master must not know, must never know, not since he foreswore his study of the Master's books, speaking bad things, using wrong words . . .

'Pay attention.'

The night before – or perhaps the night before that – Henderson had said he would no longer spend his days confined to the study, with only notes and anatomical drawings to hand; he would instead look elsewhere. the Master had said no, no, no; had insisted that Henderson – if he was to be of any *use* – must first apprentice himself by immersion in the relevant papers.

'Keep close.'

They had talked on and on, so that DogFellow's poor head had ached with the strain of trying to follow the thread, a thousand times harder than finding a scent in the woods. He tries to remember now, and can think only of the phrase *human nature*, and how the Master had first spoken of it, and Henderson had been shocked, and taken it up, exclaiming 'Surely not' and 'You can't mean . . .' DogFellow knows that the Master thinks Henderson is stupid.

'Stop daydreaming –'

DogFellow, brought back to an awareness of where he is, looks up over the high arch of the chest (mottled black and pink and yellow) to where an arm fuses with the shoulder: the stitches remain here, circumnavigating the root of the limb in a dizzying range of spirals. The flat narrowness of the belly, with its pale stropped skin, makes the rawness of the pelvis still more vivid.

'– and pay attention.'

Without purpose and without order – the Master had said that too, and he'd waved his hands about as he spoke it, as if to take in the room, the island, everything: 'And our task, if we are to have any, must be to render the world meaningful through action.' DogFellow had nodded, while Henderson floundered after, still with his talk about human nature, until the Master had shooed it away, saying, 'sentimental humbug, . . . since for all his virtues, the modern, proficient, telegraph-using citizen remains four-fifths defective, and in urgent need of – in need of . . .'

The Master lets another curl of silk drop from the surgical scissors. DogFellow looks at it. There is a knock at the door behind them. Without straightening up, the Master says, 'Yes? What is it?'

There is no answer, and then, a little muffled: 'I say, Doctor – Doctor?'

'What?'

74

'Are you busy?'

'Yes, I am.'

It is Henderson: who else? He says, 'I want to come in.'

The Master purses his mouth and lets off a controlled gust of irritation through his nose.

'I say, Doctor?'

The Master has dropped his scissors and is across the room as the door handle twists. It rattles ineffectually against the lock.

'You cannot come in here. It isn't safe. I am using chemicals which are highly volatile.'

For a moment there is no reply, until Henderson says, in a slurred voice, 'I will enter at my own risk.'

'No, you will not.'

Again, silence. Then: 'Doctor, I . . . I must protest. I really must. Your behaviour is . . . is . . .'

'What? What was that?'

He is staring at the door as if able to see through its thick planks.

'I am just saying, I cannot be expected . . . be expected to write anything . . . You are keeping things from me . . .'

DogFellow sees the back of the Master's neck colour, until it is as red as hurt flesh.

'Mr Henderson, it is *I* who cannot be expected to do my job when interrupted by damn insolent pests like you. What, have you finished your research? Have you learned what I asked you?'

'No,' says Henderson, 'Because that – that is not why I am here. You treat me like a schoolboy. I'm not your servant –'

'You are no use to me whatsoever like this,' mutters the Master.

'Listen,' says Henderson through the door, 'I did not see you this morning. I have no objection to breakfasting on my own, but, the ship – the ship will be coming very soon, in the next few days, you know that. There are things I must clarify. I am worried that I will go back and misrepresent you . . .'

DogFellow hears the lock click, sees the door half open, and the Master's head disappear.

'What is this?'

'I need to talk to you, properly.'

'It is not convenient, as I've tried to explain.'

'I am sorry, but you give me no choice. You have been shut up in here – I see no other way of getting your attention. If you – if you find my presence so intolerable, perhaps you should never have invited me.'

Briefly DogFellow glimpses Henderson's bespectacled moon face craning to get a view. Then the Master side-steps, using his big arm as a screen.

'I did not invite you,' he says. 'You invited yourself.'

Henderson waffles some reply, naming certain others who played their part in bringing about the island trip.

'I have come a long way, you know, at very consider-able expense, and while I am grateful for some of the things I have witnessed, I must repeat that I feel you are keeping things from me.'

'And I suppose a talking dog isn't miracle enough?'

Henderson puffs and pants, then says, 'What is it you have in there, on the table? I saw something move – is it the thing you have made scream? I heard it; I heard it earlier . . .'

'No. You saw nothing.'

'It is not right. I took you to be a great man, a humanitarian –'

'I want you to go away.'

'Let me look –'

To DogFellow's consternation, there is a brief scuffle, which ends in a thud as Henderson is pushed off.

'Good God, man, you have been drinking!'

'I have not,' replies Henderson tearfully, although in truth the bottle of spirits he brought in his hand luggage is now no more.

'I can smell it on you. You stink worse than a pothouse! Why, you worthless scoundrel! How dare you molest me when I am occupied –'

'You – you should not have pushed me. You've hurt my arm.'

'To the devil with your arm and with you!'

The door is slammed shut, though the Master, thin-lipped with fury, waits by it, listening. When it is opened again after a little while Henderson has crept away. The Master returns. DogFellow, agog, is brusquely brought back to his duties with a sharp word, and they resume their business as if nothing had happened, circling the creature that lies on the table. Together they work, long into the night.

Nine

Later the next day and DogFellow sees how the Master is returning Henderson's visit. Knock, knock, knock, he goes, with his big white fist on the door of the guest room, hammering loud enough to rouse the dead.

'Hey! Are you asleep? Wake up, man!'

When there is no answer the Master goes in. The American, sprawled out, blinks and instinctively reaches for his spectacles. He fumbles with the wire arms while, shirtless, he tries to sit up. His torso is white, with a tail of russet hair running down between his plumpish, pallid bosoms.

'I have been knocking for the past five minutes,' says the Master. 'I thought you must be ill.'

Henderson wonders what the time could be, wonders why the doctor is here, now. He gazes bleary-eyed as the Master squats on the room's sole chair. It creaks in protest, but the Master's expression yields nothing. The memory of their quarrel is still tangible.

Henderson starts to mumble something but the Master isn't listening.

'You look sick,' he says. 'Your complexion is sallow. The climate is to blame, of course. It saps a man's vitality, makes him weak and prone to lethargy, melancholy even. Nevertheless, it has to be said that things are always made worse and exacerbated if he conspires in sapping himself.'

'My shirt –' says Henderson. He realizes that outside the afternoon sun is still blazing. It must only be three o'clock.

'Do you know when I last emitted?'

'I beg your pardon?'

'Emitted, man, emitted.'

Henderson shakes his head.

'Seventeen years ago. Seventeen years and some months. I was not to blame, but it happened. An unforeseen provocation. Yet you may be sure that since that moment I have not lost a trace of seminal essence. Not a jot. Don't you wonder why it is I am so strong and vital, at my age, in this place?'

'I never considered it –'

'Well, you should! If you follow my example you'll keep yourself in the prime of health. When a fellow prefers idling in the shade to useful exercise then he is done for. You'll certainly be of no use to me if you continue like this. Now . . .'

'Excuse me, but before you go on I'd like to get properly dressed.'

'As you wish.'

'I need to get to my trunk.'

Ignoring all suggestions that he should leave and allow Henderson some brief respite, the Master merely gestures past himself to the further wall, where the trunk rests. Henderson rises and goes to rummage through his clothes, until he finds a fresh garment. He puts it on and does up the buttons. The Master watches. He says:

'You are wondering why I'm here. Rest assured that I have not come to exact any kind of apology. Let your own conscience reproach you with that. I have no wish to discuss the matter further. However, I do wish to discuss this.'

For the first time Henderson notices that the Master is holding a leather-covered notebook in his hand.

'Is it – is that mine?' he asks, too startled to be angry.

'Yes. I took it to read through, and I'm very glad I did.'

'When?'

'Earlier. It hardly matters.'

Henderson opens and shuts his mouth a few times before saying, 'You had no right to do that. Those are private jottings.'

'I don't think so. Not given the content, and the proof it gives that you have looked to inveigle yourself into this house as a spy. As an assassin.'

The Master's bland expression does not change, even as his words grow violent.

'Doctor, I must protest –'

'Protest? I think that is my prerogative, Mr Henderson.'

He holds the notebook as if weighing its contents.

'Poison. Poisonous rubbish. Every page, every line. I've read it all, from end to end, so there is no point in denial.'

'This is nonsense . . .'

'You think I am so unworldly that I don't know your kind?'

'What? What kind?'

'Go and sit back down. Sit down, Mr Henderson.'

Despite his rising colour the American does as he is told.

'You are no different from the rest,' says the Master. 'I thought perhaps, with your different accent, your clothes, your lack of manners, there might be a corresponding absence of bile, of spite. The more fool I. I have known you all my life. You drove me to this place.'

'I assure you I have absolutely no idea what you're talking about.'

'Envy. The tyranny of little men. You dare stand in judgement over me?'

'Of course not –'

'What you have written in this book tells me otherwise. You still deny it? Let me look.'

He begins to sort through the pages.

'For God's sake,' Henderson declares, 'they are only the roughest kind of notes. You can set no stock by them. Let me have it back –'

And he is about to come across, and take it by main force if necessary, except the Master glances up and says 'Sit down, I tell you!' in such a manner that the other man falls back heavily on his bed and stares, half embarrassed and half angry.

'Here,' says the Master, 'and I quote. "He is king and emperor, such as may only be found surviving in China, or some barbarous African kingdom." And then, on the page opposite, "Where will it end; what boundaries; no boundaries; no spirit, no ethics; man cultivated like a chrysanthemum; something something" – I can't read it – then – ha! "mad, mad" – or it might be "made" – your damned handwriting is a disgrace – and on it goes, page after page of sly insinuating trash. Here again: "Monsters!" That is what you have written – there – you deny the evidence of your own eyes?'

He holds the notebook up, to show the page and the heading, underlined three times.

'They're idle scribbles, that's all. No more than that,' says Henderson, unable to keep a tremor out of his voice.

'It is a betrayal!' shouts the Master, and he randomly tears out a sheaf of paper, and casts the rest back at the American, hitting him in the chest. 'You dare to peddle this rubbish! What, did you think to sail away from here, and noise it abroad that I am some species of lunatic despot? You think I would ever allow it?'

'No! No, of course not. I – I swear there is no malice in what I have written. I swear it, on the bible. And if you have read these pages, then you must be aware that for every expression of scepticism there are a dozen that give full acknowledgement to your genius. You are a genius, sir. A great genius.'

'Hmmmph!' says the Master. Then he says, 'Nevertheless, it is plain to me that you have not understood what I have told you. You have not understood my work. You are running the terrible risk of having wasted your time in coming here.'

'Forgive me, sir,' says Henderson, 'but you must remember, that what I have written – and what I will go on to write – is intended to edify and inform the readership of the newspaper I write for. My editors have paid for me to come here. I am, in large measure, beholden to them, and to the many thousands of men and women who are eager to learn of what you do, and your great – your truly great – achievements.'

'I don't give a damn for their opinion,' he is told, brusquely. 'So far as we need concern ourselves, I am your audience. It is me who you write for. To the devil with your editors. Who's feeding you and putting a roof over your head?'

A look of utter exasperation crosses Henderson's face.

'But surely – before I even arrived – you had some inkling as to the nature of my calling –'

'You are a professional writer; that is all that mattered then, or matters now. It is all that need concern us.'

'Sir, this is entirely unreasonable of you –'

'Ssh. Be quiet a moment.'

The Master leans back in his chair, then bellows: 'Dog-Fellow!'

A moment later and DogFellow's head appears at the door. He has loitered outside through all the shouting and the stamping, and now is told to go and fetch some tea.

'A little refreshment,' says the Master, his fury altogether passed, his manner now inclining to the philosophic. He pulls his favourite briar pipe out of his jacket pocket and turns it about in his hands. He is silent for a long while, then says, 'The greatest favour you could perform for these readers of yours – for all readers; I mean the readers of the world – would be to take this notebook and any others you have filled, and set about kindling a small fire. I will supply you with a match.'

Henderson swallows hard.

'But what then should I have to take back with me?'

The Master points his pipe stem at the man.

'We must remedy the lack by working together. Perhaps I am in some measure at fault, in leaving you unsupervised till now. Well, no matter. I have finished my business. I am here. I am yours. A couple of weeks and we may have hammered out something more in keeping with what I have done.'

'Well, sir,' says Henderson, 'I am grateful, don't think I'm not – I only wish it could have been this way from the start – but it's an unfortunate fact that I will be leaving in four days' time, so there just won't be the opportunity for us to be so ambitious.'

'Is it so close?' replies the Master, rapping the upturned pipe bowl against his palm.

'Yes sir. Five days at the outside. I was told the boat could be twelve hours late – something to do with the current –'

'Oh, but I should not be so sanguine about any imminent departure if I were you. Our friend van Toch is not the most reliable of seafarers.'

'What do you mean?'

'You must learn patience, Mr Henderson, along with a few other things beside.'

'I am to be ready to go in four days – that is, the

twenty-sixth of the month – I have the bill of passage that the company drafted . . .'

And Henderson would turn it out, except at that moment DogFellow appears, bearing an ancient silver tray heavy with tea things, which he sets down on the table.

'Do you have a pencil?' the Master asks.

Mechanically Henderson says, 'I've a pen. In my jacket pocket.'

'Get it. And find yourself a fresh piece of paper. Come on, man; we only have an hour of daylight left. Time is pressing, as you have made abundantly plain.'

DogFellow pours the tea while Henderson quickly gathers up his writing kit.

'It's for the best if I simply give you a few basic facts and you write it down, word for word. So . . .'

But instead of speaking the Master falls silent for a minute or more, his head bowed forward, and his powerful smooth hands pressed together.

'You have put today's date?' he finally asks.

Henderson nods, taking the cup and saucer he is silently offered.

'Put the time as well. It's a quarter past four.'

While Henderson scribbles the Master mutters 'Precision, precision'. Then, in a loud voice, as if suddenly addressing a lecture audience, he begins.

Ten

It is the hour after they have eaten, these beast people: an hour at least before the Master will be sitting down in expectation of his supper; and DogFellow lingers by the water trough, slyly watching Fantine. She has a cup, of course (although its handle is missing), yet she leaves it on the stone ledge as she bends forward, as if to wet her face. As she does so a second Fantine appears and for long moments they cling together by the motion of their tongues and lips while, without shame, the water is lapped up. DogFellow emits a low whine and claps his hand to the side of his head. She continues to drink, but her eyes are on him. She stops and stands up, licking water droplets off her lips. The front of her vest is damp. The sight of her like this disturbs DogFellow.

'Don't you like to drink?' she asks him.

He shows his cup with a certain defiance. She laughs, and the sound floats like a leaf on the noise of the water.

'Ah, DogFellow, you are so serious always.'

'It is the Law,' he mumbles, as if describing the reason

for his demeanour; but he means, in his awkward way, to rebuke her, and to show how a thirst ought to be slaked. Feeling foolish he dashes his cup into the water and drinks it off, even though he has no want of it.

'There,' he says, with a gasp.

'And now I know.'

She smiles at him.

'You show us the way, DogFellow.'

He stares, understanding that her words bear more than a surface meaning.

'Do not be cross with me,' she says. 'You are the best at knowing things. I will use my cup. See?'

She imitates his actions, catching a swirl of water and sipping at it. Whatever vexed DogFellow is washed away. He feels a sudden stupid flush of pleasure and wants to keep her there to talk some more.

'The Law is not so hard to remember,' he says.

She has green eyes and her teeth are small and sharp and as white as coconut flesh.

'Ah, but now we have two Masters,' she says. 'Some of us cannot make sense of it. Who is best?'

DogFellow looks perplexed, though he tries not to show it.

'Why, our Master of course,' he says. 'He made us. He loves us. He – he cares for us.'

'So what does this other Master do?'

'He helps our Master. He . . .'

DogFellow tries to picture Henderson at his tasks: Henderson, with his red hair bowed down over the table, glimpsed now and then when the door is ajar.

'He writes,' he says at last. 'Night and day. He makes pages and pages, to tell about our Master.'

Fantine stands on one leg. With her other foot she caresses the back of her slender calf.

'Hmm, yes,' she says. 'I have seen that.'

'What do you mean?'

'I went to the house. I looked through the window. He knocked on the glass at me.'

DogFellow is consternated.

'You must not! It is forbidden to –'

She laughs.

'You are so serious! I did not do it. But I will, if you will go with me . . .'

'No!'

'Let me look and see DogFellow. While the Master is busy.'

'No!'

'I want to look at the other Master. He is strange. Where does he come from?'

'I cannot say.'

'What does he write?'

'It is a secret. I have not seen anything.'

'Then who is it he is going to tell about our Master?'

DogFellow, already brought to the edge of orthodoxy, shakes his head.

'These are bad questions.'

'But you have answers.'

Yet what answers can he give? Only that when the two Masters are together, usually for a time in the evenings, there are mutterings vaguely audible in the corridor

outside, and sometimes – of late, often – it is not necessary to creep up close to catch the sudden squalls of rage
and angry rejoinders. The Master, Henderson; Henderson,
the Master, backwards and forwards, like a spider knitting
its web. When does this other Master ever leave off his
scribing and come out? DogFellow only understands that
the food must be left outside the door on a plate, and once
a day the bucket, with its odoriferous stew of yellow and
brown, must be taken, swilled clean, and brought back.
Perhaps at night Henderson emerges, along with the moths
which throng the tropical darkness. DogFellow does not
know, but he knows he does not like it.

'You are the only one who can tell,' says Fantine.

He feels the blood rising in his face. He is a head taller
than her. In the evening air he can smell her, take in
the flavour of her scent, which is quite different from the
familiar odours of the damp earth and the sea.

'You must not keep secrets, DogFellow.'

'I do not,' he says, but he does not sound convincing,
even to himself.

'Come with me,' she says. 'We can walk together. I
know a place where there are grubs this big.'

She holds her thumb and index finger three inches
apart. He hesitates, and at that moment, from behind,
there comes the crackle of twigs being broken.

'Who's there?' he calls out.

'No one. There's no one,' says Fantine.

She comes a step nearer.

'I must go,' says DogFellow.

He feels as if he has just been woken out of a senseless doze.

'The Master . . .'

'What?'

'The Master! His dinner. Goodbye.'

And, in the manner of a startled fish, DogFellow darts away as fast as his crooked legs will carry him.

When he gets back to the compound there is a fearful rush to heat the griddle and prepare the squid, which has to be gutted and cut into pieces.

As he is easing out the ink sac over a china bowl he senses that the Master is standing in the doorway of the kitchen pantry.

'Don't make too much,' he is gruffly told.

DogFellow nervously puts down his little knife.

'Enough for me only.'

The limp tentacles of the squid lie tangled with his own fingers.

'Is the other Master sick?' he asks.

A tiny reflex action of the great bearded jaw – the chink of molars at the back of the mouth – communicates to DogFellow that he has erred in his remark and must endure the consequences, which are not slow in following.

'What did you call him?'

Turning about, DogFellow says, 'The other – Master –'

'You damned fool! How dare you!'

He takes a step forward into the narrow space, and DogFellow flinches, instinctively foreseeing a cuff to the head. However, the great white hands – the left, which gives pain; the right, which brings felicity – hang immobile.

'How many Masters do you think you have?'

Peering forlornly at that angry face, DogFellow stutters out that he has one only.

'One only – one only – what, is that so difficult to remember, idiot?'

'No.'

'Forget it again and I'll open you up like that thing you've got in your paw. That other person does not exist. Get it into your head. Don't make me force it in there. There is no one in this house apart from me. There is no Henderson, and there certainly is no other Master. Other Master – Christ!'

Then he stops and goes off, muttering.

When later he is brought his solitary dinner he looks at the glistening strips of flesh and the slightly singed tentacles curled into knots and he shakes his head.

'Take it away. It looks disgusting.'

Wanting only to obey, DogFellow leaves with the dish.

'And you're disgusting too!' comes the cry, at his back. 'You disgust me. All of you – all of you disgust me.'

Eleven

More than a week goes by and then, while he is busily
sweeping the yard, he hears a voice calling to him, low and
hoarse with desperation. Because DogFellow has been
daydreaming he is briefly caught offguard and does not
show the rectitude he should. His eyes swivel to the point
of disturbance and he notices how Henderson has contrived to prise out a couple of slats from the shutter that
has been blanking out his window. Pressing his mouth to
the gap he calls again.

'Hey you! I know you can hear me. Don't turn your
back to me. Come closer. Closer! I need to speak to you.
Here . . .'

The American utters a series of soft, amorphous
sounds, designed he evidently thinks to tempt DogFellow,
in the way a parrot or half-feral creature might be tempted
to take food from a human hand. DogFellow of course is
not of that mettle. And yet he does not move, nor does he
turn away, as he ought. Henderson is paler and unshaven,
his chops and chin now shaded with a gingerish scurf. His

face is too big to fit the vent he's made, and so his head bobs up and down, framing his mouth and then his eyes, which, despite being fenced off by pebbles of glass, still possess a piercing, angry power.

'Now you listen to me,' he says, in a stage whisper, 'if you don't come here right now you are going to be very sorry. I have something very important to tell you. Come here. Come on.'

Realizing, by virtue of DogFellow's immobility, that this will not work, Henderson changes his method and his tone of voice.

'Look, look –'

He disappears altogether for a moment and then his hand is extruded through the hole, clasping a piece of fish skin with a hank of fin stuck to it.

'Here,' he hisses, 'this is for you, come closer so you can have it . . .'

There is a pause.

'Damn you, you stupid bloody brute! Get here or I swear I'll climb out there and give you such a whipping!'

DogFellow is as unmoved by threats as he is by suspect scraps. Still, he lingers on, watching the antics of one he knows has been ruled out of existence. Henderson continues to stare back, with his glassy eyes and ginger face.

'All right, all right,' he says, wiping at his mouth. 'Maybe you don't want to speak. That's all right. I don't want you to get into trouble with him. I want – I want to help you. To help us both. If – if you want to just stay there and listen to what I've got to say that's fair enough. Yes –

yes, it's all all right. Just so long as I know that you can hear me –'

There is a sudden catch in Henderson's throat and he swallows before continuing.

'Just listen. What the doctor is doing in keeping me here is a crime. I am being held against my will, and that is against the law. When the people who sent me here find out they are going to be very, very angry. They will send a boat here, with soldiers and . . . and policemen, and other people, very important people, you wouldn't understand, but understand this – that man and everyone else who helps him will be going to prison for a very long time. He may even get the death sentence, or be sent to work in a quarry for the rest of his life. Yes! Or a chain gang, digging ditches. What do you think about that?'

Henderson wipes at the sweat on his face with a dirty white handkerchief.

'Now, bearing in mind what I just said, and if you want to help me – to help yourself – you'll find out when the next ship is due here. I've been on this island now for forty-one days, or forty-two, I can't be sure. There must be a ship due soon, I know there must. Find out when, and . . .'

Henderson falters and coughs to clear his throat.

'Can't you find that out for me? Nod. Just nod, that's all I ask.'

DogFellow does nothing other than continue to stare mutely. Henderson heaves a sigh.

'I know you understand everything I say. Perhaps you're too afraid to answer. I can appreciate that. He's filled your head with all kinds of lunatic ideas. He tells you he's the be-all and end-all, Jesus Christ almighty come back to earth, living and ruling here, in the middle of nowhere, where nobody can tell him to stop. Oh, I can see you've suffered. I hear screams, coming out of the place where he works, sometimes at night, sometimes in the middle of the day. I've never heard anything to match that, I can tell you, not in the Philippines, not in Cuba. What is war compared to this? He's a sadistic bloody butcher all right. No, don't answer. Say nothing. You don't have to nod. I realize you understand my – our – our situation. So listen to me. Just listen. This can all end. You could be free, you and every one of your friends. You don't have to be slaves. You can all live as men, proper men and women. Believe me! This place where we are, it's not the world. It isn't even on the charts! Where I come from – a great country, far away, you can – you can . . .'

Exhausted by the effort of his frenzied talk – part exposition, part advertisement, part plea – Henderson stops. He disappears and then reappears, holding up his hand. There is a square of paper folded between his fingers.

'I've written down what I want you to do. You can read, can't you? Yes, of course you can. He told me, that very first night. Take this and hide it. Look it over when you have the chance.'

The paper whisks in an arc and goes past DogFellow to drop on to the swept sand.

'Pick it up, pick it up!' says Henderson, in a frenzy. 'Quickly, go and get it before he comes out and finds it. Don't let him find it! And don't forget what I told you; you can go free, leave this place, escape with me . . . Go on, go on. Pick it up!'

As if half asleep DogFellow brings his broom around and bats the illicit scribble away from himself, knocking it back the way it came, so that it ends up nestling against the wall of the house.

'Oh for God's sake –' exclaims Henderson and says no more, retreating back into the room that has become a cell, perhaps to lie despairing on the bed, or else to pour his heart out in further forbidden scribbling.

DogFellow sees that he has gone, sees the end of his brush and the swirl it has fashioned across the dusty ground, sees also, out of the corner of his eye, the folded paper.

If Henderson does not exist, can anything from his hand have any purchase on the surface of the world? No, DogFellow tells himself: it does not exist either, and thinking this thought he goes off to draw a bucket of water.

Twelve

But the very next day Henderson is gone. DogFellow, laundering bandages and bed sheets, can see the shutter thrown wide, its gap repaired. The room itself is dim and empty. Trundling his barrow across the yard, he finds them both standing by the door, smoking cigarettes. Henderson looks better, though he remains unshaven. He breaks off from his muttered replies to study DogFellow. DogFellow, afraid, keeps his gaze directed on the copper wash pot, which bubbles and steams in the corner of the compound, to the left of the main gate. The Master is talking about the way he put the palisade in place by hand, toiling up the beach with eight-foot lathes of timber strapped to his back.

'Sounds like awful hard work,' says Henderson, drawing his cigarette down to the quick and sending puffs of smoke out of his nose.

'The strongest things are forged in adversity,' observes the Master. After the fence they pass on to a history of the house from the foundations up, with a careful enumeration of all the troubles that flowed from the unreliability and general worthlessness of Captain Hughes, who predated J. van Toch as main supplier. Henderson nods and gives the occasional taut smile, while observing the way Dog-Fellow works, steering his handcart backwards and forwards. The Master continues talking and simultaneously extracts two more cigarettes from his pocket, lighting both on the stub he still holds in the corner of his mouth. He hands one to Henderson and explains that to get a better appreciation of the roof (half tiled and half thatched) they will need to go out a little way and take a turn about the walls. Henderson, attacking his new smoke with all the avidity expended on the last, falls in behind the Master's purposeful stride. They cut across DogFellow's path. The Master pays him no more attention than would be accorded to the bandages piled up in the barrow, but Henderson stares hard, and without wanting it DogFellow is snared up behind those pebble lenses and the red-rimmed eyes burn him. They disappear out through the gate.

He does not know what this means. He ought to be glad: the shouting and the locked door disturbed him greatly. But he is frightened of Henderson, as if Henderson, with his murky irises, can see even what the Master has not discovered, though the Master made DogFellow, and surely crafted every thought that the head can conceive of.

He tries not to think, considering only the swirl and skirmishing of suds at the top of the copper pot. The pot sits on bricks; the bricks make a chamber, and into this sticks must be fed, to keep the fire burning. Next to it stands a little hut, where the sticks are kept in bundles, and there is a big carton of soda flakes, and other necessities. DogFellow repairs there, to sit and wait and watch the steam rising.

An hour goes by and still there is silence. The fire is put out. The water is allowed to cool. Carefully – this part is always very awkward – he tips the copper, so that half the water runs out. With a stick he begins to lift out the sheets and, after a cursory wring, lets them flop into his barrow.

'What are you doing?'

Henderson, who has reappeared on his own from around the corner of the stockade, addresses DogFellow.

'I said, what are you doing?'

Where is the Master? DogFellow glances from the cauldron, with its still-steaming dregs, to the stick in his hand, and from this towards the hand barrow, already half piled up with freshly boiled linen, as if by these connected glances everything will be revealed, and Henderson satisfied. But Henderson is not satisfied, and again says, 'What are you doing there?'

DogFellow, suspicious and fearful, waves his stick, on which a clout is hanging, and he dips his head at the open mouth of the pot. He is relieved when Henderson half nods.

'Another one of your chores, I see. Do you have to do this every day?'

DogFellow, in the act of reaching his stick down to hook the remaining sheet, covertly grimaces. Then he draws it out and mutters 'No,' before twitching his stick one last time and readying himself to push the barrow away.

'It seems like a lot of trouble. Difficult if you're all by yourself.'

Henderson talks as if he had not heard DogFellow's gruff reply and then he comes over. He is not tall and straight like the Master, but plump and round-shouldered. DogFellow, seeing Henderson stoop to reach the edge of the barrow, draws it back and wheels it round.

'What's the matter?' asks Henderson, with a surprised grin.

'Not to touch,' says DogFellow, though without conviction.

'Why not?' asks Henderson, still grinning.

'Master said no.'

'Ah yes,' says Henderson, his grin hardening.

DogFellow wants to get by but Henderson is standing in the way.

'Stay a while. Don't try and push past.'

DogFellow attempts to bear his barrow to the right. Henderson raises his foot and sets it against the wheel.

'There's no need to run away. You didn't try and run away before.'

His voice is lowered and he glances over his shoulder before continuing to speak.

'I wanted to thank you for not letting on about that: about what we talked about yesterday. I appreciate the gesture. If he knew I'd never have been let out like this. So, thanks.'

His hand is extended. After a few moments he drops it.

'The fact is,' continues Henderson, 'I need a friend pretty badly. Someone just like you, DogFellow. *Dog-Fellow*: that is your name, isn't it?'

DogFellow feels a sudden, crawling kind of heat pass over him.

'No,' he says.

'No?'

'No name.'

'I don't believe you,' says Henderson. 'If you're a man you must have a name. You're a man, aren't you?'

DogFellow stays silent.

'Perhaps you'd prefer something different. You choose.'

There is the far-off chatter of beasts, returning from the fields.

'DogFellow,' says DogFellow, almost inaudibly.

'Good. I'm glad we got that straightened out.' Henderson shakes his head. 'I must say this has all turned into quite a story. Perhaps I'll take you back with me. It's the only way that they'll believe this place exists. You ready for an ocean trip?'

DogFellow can hear his own heart. The beat is strong and powerful.

'Off the island. Away from this place. Understand? I can't stay for much longer, you should know that. I realize I'm supposed to be in situ until I get the good doctor's manifesto word-perfect, but it's not going to work out that way. You don't mind me sharing these things, do you? I feel I can trust you. So tell me: did you ever stop to wonder what might lie beyond the far horizon? Now that's what really separates the men from the dogs.'

There is no reply. Henderson gives a sigh and looks away, but as he turns to go DogFellow says, in a clear voice, 'Paris.'

'What ?'

'Paris. In Paris,' repeats DogFellow. His legs are trembling. He steadies himself by gripping tightly to the handles of his barrow. 'There is a place. Not here. I know. I . . .' He tongue falls lame. He can't find the words.

Henderson nods encouragingly. 'Oh yes, Paris.' He pronounces it as a Frenchman would. 'I've always wanted to go there myself. The city of light, the seat of reason. How did you learn about that? Was it from your Master?'

DogFellow, led on by feelings he cannot understand, begins to shake his head, then stops.

'Well, maybe we can arrange it. But first we've got to get back home. My home that is. Could be your home as well. Have you heard of the United States?'

'No.'

'That's too bad. You'd enjoy it, my friend. The land of opportunity. Get you a decent tailor, a trip to the barbers, put your name on the electoral roll. Make a citizen out of you.'

'A citi-zen?'

The last syllable buzzes between his tongue and teeth. It makes him think of *civilization*.

'And why not?' says Henderson, and he looks away, to blink the sweat out of his eyes. It is as if the spell is broken.

A sudden and powerful sense of wrong comes over DogFellow. With a lurch to the right he passes around the obstructive foot and heads for the open gate.

'Hey!'

Head down, bumping his front wheel over a stone, DogFellow keeps trundling.

'Don't go – we have to talk some more!'

Henderson says something else, calling out to him, but he does not look back, and he does not listen.

Thirteen

Later – and he has finished his tasks for the day and would go, returning to the world of the huts and his fellow beasts, except the Master is not inclined to dismiss him. So he waits in the yard, thinking to himself about *Paris* and *citizen*, and in time is startled to smell the odours of frying fish and hear the disconcerting sound of men's voices raised not in argument but convivial chatter.

He dares to rise out of his squat and cock one ear to the back and forth of words, first the Master and then Henderson, the latter growing in mirth and volubility minute by minute. It is as it was before, when Henderson first came to this place – as if the shouting and the locked door and the contempt and anger of each for the other was nothing but writing etched in wet sand, now smoothed flat by the roll of the surf, as if none of it had ever been. And what if there should be two Masters again, like twin suns, or double moons? It taxes DogFellow to consider such a possibility and yet, he thinks, better that it be so, for in the reconfiguration of both men there seems to lie a curious peace, deadening the terrible unease he feels.

Hearing the Master's tread he backs out of his alert pose, feigning a doze. For a moment he thinks he has been forgotten but then, slowly, the door opens. No light shows itself: the Master stands in darkness, looking into darkness. When he speaks it is in a hoarse whisper, emptied entirely of the ripe joviality with which he has been buttering his dinner guest.

'Are you there?'

'Yes,' says DogFellow.

'Shhh! Keep your voice down. Come here.'

DogFellow shuffles forward. The door is only half open. Behind the Master, up the hall and to the left, there is the clatter of knife and fork and the faintest flicker of a lamp, but he is a hulking shadow, rumbling secrets.

'You must go to the infirmary and fetch my leather valise. It will be by the stool, in the corner. Bring it back. I'll leave the door off the latch. Put it down here, where I'm standing, savvy? Then you can come into the dining room. Go, do it now. Don't make any mistakes.'

The Master says nothing else and steps back inside. The sky is moonless tonight. DogFellow wishes he had a candle as he crosses the cool dirt. It is not that he is unfamiliar with the way – how could he be? – yet he is afraid. The house of sickness means only bad luck. With a rising thud in his chest he reaches its tin portal and draws the bolt. The squeak is loud and finds an echo from behind the white canvas partition that hangs, like some geometrically exact ghost, across half the room. DogFellow holds his breath: to draw in even a moiety of the infected air will bring illness and disaster, he is quite sure. In the dark he feels his way to the place the Master has indicated. The bag is half undone and terribly heavy to lift. Deep inside it, metal strikes metal. Again he hears an answering cry, coming out from behind the divide, where the bunks with the leather ties and the iron bars are. He stifles a gasp of effort that might undo the tight seal he has set between his lips and nose. The odour is already upon him, of course, but once he's back outside its withering stink will lose power. Yet he cannot plug his ears to the sounds. Near the door, as he struggles to get a full purchase on the leather case, the whining transmutes itself to a loud and terrible groan, accompanied by the rattle of wooden joints. He is compelled to picture someone, something, chained and cut from head to toe, and he is so desperate to be on his way that he stumbles and drops his load in the dust. The whole world must be alert! From behind him the groan has passed to something else, inchoate but querulous, and then angry: a furious, slobbering growl, as if the tormentor was already standing by the torture bed, with knife and hook at hand. DogFellow wants to run but steadies himself and bolts the door shut, smelling the smell.

He picks up the bag and, recrossing the yard, enters the house, gratefully leaving it where the Master explained. He can already hear him at his feast, proposing a toast to the marriage of letters and science: his words big and grand and resonating all along the hallway.

Slowly DogFellow goes to the source, trying to give some respite to his poor, overworked heart. The scent of fish and fried sweet potato hangs heavy on the slightly stale air, misted with tobacco smoke. DogFellow feels a gust of nausea pull at him. He knocks before entering, trying not to look in Henderson's direction at all.

'. . . and for this reason,' says the Master, with only a flicker of the eyes, 'we must push as hard as we can to ensure a thorough accommodation between our two professions. It is no longer a case of gentleman amateurs and occasional scribes. We are on the threshold of a whole new age. I think we're agreed?'

'Absolutely,' says Henderson, the second syllable turning slushy on his dark-stained tongue. He is halfway through a fifth glass of wine.

'Then let us shake, let us shake.'

DogFellow takes a step or two to the wall as the Master lumbers up from his seat, his big flat hand extended to swallow up Henderson's own. The grasp is held for seconds as the Master beams.

'I am immensely glad that you feel as I do.'

'Always did, Doc,' says Henderson, focusing on the swollen white bulbs of his host's knuckles.

'Which therefore only proves how easily misunderstandings may arise. It ought to be a lesson to all the statesmen of the world, whether president, king or kaiser.'

'You can be sure it will,' says Henderson.

'Yes,' says the Master, finally releasing his hand clasp. He returns to his seat. 'Come and clear the table,' he says to DogFellow.

The two men lean back and watch as needles of bone and tatters of skin are awkwardly scraped off the plates.

'Now, would you care for a little brandy?'

Even before Henderson can reply that he would, the Master is up again and fussing about the doors of the small rosewood corner cabinet which has stoutly resisted the corrosion of a tropical climate for nearly twenty years.

'Ahh,' he says, 'I left it in the other room,' and with a mutter he goes out. DogFellow, finished with scraping, sets the dirty cutlery in parallel across the top plate, in an agony lest Henderson says so much as a word, but silence reigns, save for the man's heavy breathing. Henderson's cheeks are pink; his mouth is red. He belches unselfconsciously and gives a noisy sniff.

In the hall outside the tinny chimes of the clock count up to ten and with a bang the Master returns, a dark bottle under the crook of his arm and two fresh glasses already charged with double measures in each fist.

'Hurry up with that, you lazy devil,' he mutters to DogFellow as he gives one glass to Henderson and raises his own. By the light of the candelabrum the brandy possesses a deep amber shade. 'When you are able to return to America –' he begins.

'I hope that it will be soon,' says Henderson, suddenly pulled out of the doze that was descending on him.

'Yes, yes, within a fortnight, rest assured,' says the Master. 'And when you return, I hope you will be able to explain how all that I've attempted here – everything, down to the least little action – has been actuated by the highest – the very highest – motives. I have been subject to no selfish or partisan interests –'

'I'm going to go on the very next ship and tell them just that.'

'– no selfish motives. Reputation is of immense importance in the everyday world. My name must be favourably represented. People must see – must appreciate . . .'

Here he falters, as if surprised by the emotion in his voice.

'Absolutely, Doc, no question about that. And don't worry that we haven't quite got all the writing finished. I'm going to make sure I get it all polished up on the way home, and ready to go straight to press.'

'I'm entirely at your mercy,' says the Master, a trifle coquettish.

'You and me together. It's my reputation too you know – as much my name as yours. The sooner you can fix up my passage out of here the sooner I can let everyone know about what you've done on this island.'

The Master dips his head, as if blushing.

'You really are too kind, too kind. Your good health.'

They raise their glasses and drink. Henderson splutters.

'Are you quite all right?' he is asked.

Henderson rubs the back of his neck and nods, smiling.

'It's an excellent brandy, more than thirty years old. I had a quantity given to me as a student. This is the very last of it. I can imagine no better end than using it to bless tonight's proceedings.'

And he talks on, while DogFellow roves back and forth, taking out plates and dirty spoons and desultory platters. When he has finished, he is ready to go, but the Master shakes his head and so he waits, the stationary mute, listening to the flow of words, the current swirling round and round the theme of faces and (more especially) the trials the Master has been through in turning the muddy commonplaces of the animal kingdom to higher ends.

'In my own head,' he says, 'I carry the Greek ideal. I think of that marvellous bust of Pericles. Do you know it? I have it illustrated by a plate in one of the history books. But I don't need to go and bring it in. It's engraved upon my mind's eye. A splendid piece, a face of the most noble character: high brow, straight nose, perfect symmetry between all the features, a fine dolichocephalic skull – clear supraorbital development – quite extraordinary. Another great benefactor of the human race, Mr Henderson. If the world's foremost artists, physiologists, phrenologists, were to meet in conclave to design the ideal of human perfection I cannot see how they could improve upon it in any particular whatsoever. Do you follow?'

Henderson nods mechanically.

'Naturally, one could never consider such a face, such a head, to be beautiful, but what is more contemptible than beauty in the male? If we are to recast the human species it must be founded upon the rock of fortitude, of virile endeavour. The Greeks came very near to it two and a half millennia ago. I talk of the old Greeks, of course. The modern sort . . . well. You take my point?'

There is a slight pause between Henderson unhitching

his jaw and engaging his tongue, but then he says, 'Yes, shurely.'

'So, I was inevitably drawn to the Pericles, which you might consider excessively ambitious, but I quickly appreciated that its perfection lies in its total simplicity. It could be etched in a few lines. It is ugliness that is complicated.'

Though he himself is barely conscious of the gesture, his eyes are momentarily drawn from the vacancy of Henderson's bibulous stare towards the singular concoction standing unobtrusively in the corner, with its sutured nose, sloping forehead and hopelessly manufactured top lip.

'Ugliness, 'he repeats, a little ruefully. 'However, even in this there is a vindication of one's ideals. I had to labour to turn the abject sameness of this brute or that into something recognizably human. You see him, waiting patiently over there?'

Henderson does not, because his own eyes have started to glaze over. The Master continues anyway.

'He can never revert to what he has been, to find anonymity, the anonymity of the pack. Everything else I've touched has made the same journey, crossing the divide. Think of it as a river. On one side there are herds milling about, senseless and careless – an undifferentiated organic mass. The vast majority stay as they are, but a few – a very few – tumble into the water and swim clear, and as they swim they are transformed. Up the other bank they crawl, herd animals no longer, to rest panting in the sun. A poetic image, you'll agree. I think of it often.'

He sits back and traces around the rim of his brandy glass with his big, flat-ended index finger.

'Where once you would only find mere instinct, geared to the rudiments of alimentation, slumber and the seasonal rut, now you may discover a mirror of your own self, an authentic mind, capable of playing host to every thought that buzzes about your own head, in the middle of the day and sometimes in the small hours of the night. I have given twenty years of my life to achieve these things. How long did it take Nature to make the same? You are beginning to drool, Mr Henderson.'

A bubble of spit forms and pops in the corner of Henderson's mouth, but he seems oblivious to it.

'I can see I have worn you out. Perhaps the drink is stronger than your constitution will allow. An extra-special vintage, as I said. Now, where was I? Ah, yes. Human expression and its re-creation by artificial means. Do you have any inkling as to how many muscles are engaged in producing a furrowed brow? Perhaps you've never considered it. Now, there is an apposite book on the subject, by the great Darwin; it was published almost as an afterthought, in the wake of his *Descent of Man* –'

With a sudden gurgle Henderson's upper body flops sideways, causing the chair to tip. DogFellow flinches as the momentum brings chair and man crashing over on to the carpet. The Master is unmoved.

'Well, that took its time,' he says.

Henderson starts to snore very loudly. DogFellow sees how pale he has become, and the dark gape of his open mouth. One of his arms lies flung out. The Master remains where he is, until the clock in the hall, striking the half hour, recalls him from his reverie. He rubs his beard and, pushing back his chair, goes about to stand over the body.

'Lift his feet so that they don't drag,' he says.

Since DogFellow is the only possible presence that could sensibly carry out such a request he steps forward. Seizing hold of Henderson as if he were no more than a throttled chicken the Master half turns him, rolling him on to his back.

The snoring grows still louder. Perhaps the American is already off on his journey home, across the sea, where fame awaits.

'We're going to take him to the stone room,' explains the Master, getting a good grip under Henderson's armpits. DogFellow bends to grasp the thin, sockless ankles. Together they shuffle along, down the hall, out of the back door, across the yard and out through the gates.

Their destination lies squat by the northern wall of the palisade, where the sun is kept in some kind of abeyance. It consists of the crudest conceivable assemblage of blackened pumice and coral blocks, cemented together and raised up to make a cube six feet wide and eight feet deep, with a rough but thick roof of woven palm leaves and wooden planking. The inside is dank and malodorous, despite a recent fumigation. It is a place of death, where those creatures that expire in transit across the Master's imaginary river can lie until the secret of their failure might be teased out of them. Tonight, however, DogFellow and the Master want accommodation for the living.

Snoring loudly, Henderson is tied hand and foot and

left to slumber on the dirt while the door is shut behind him.

'None of this ever happened,' says the Master, as they walk back to the house.

The very next day a ship appears off the island.

Sitting by the water, he stared at the way it shimmered, holding him upside down. He reached out to tug at the stray hairs that colonized his cheekbones, and his image dissolved into ribbons of dusky light and movement. With two hands he dashed water into his face. He wetted the back of his neck and then washed his arms up past the elbow, very thoroughly.

However, he had come down to this place to perform more than his ablutions. First he had to be patient, for the sun was still rising and in the absence of their dawn ritual (obsolete for many months) the beast people came and went indifferently. He suspected that some did not get up at all until the heat of the sun lured them down to the sea's edge. There had been a terrible unravelling. DogFellow knew it and it grieved him. Yet even the most purblind of individuals – a Slope for instance – must feel a quickening at the dreadful things DogFellow had discovered. He thought back to the beginning, drawing grim satisfaction from the horror manifest in Lemura's own report, telling of Hector and Fantine and their contempt for the word of the Master. Who would not shudder to learn of it? thought DogFellow.

After drying himself with a square of sun-bleached cloth, he retreated to a natural seat, caused by the partial collapse of a stone wall built to square off the washing troughs. The path that led to this place lay to DogFellow's left. The need to press through overgrown bushes would tell him at once whether anyone approached. And so he sat and waited, unafraid – indeed, he was eager and his busy hands snapped at the little lizards that ran in and out of cracks in the stonework. After a while – he reckoned it at half an hour, though his sense of the passing of hours and minutes was less acute than he would admit – he heard a great crackling of branches and a rattling of leaves. He did not stand but folded his arms and gazed fixedly forward as the bulk of BearCreature appeared on the path. DogFellow wished that it was not him, but then pushing aside all footling apprehensions, called out 'Hello!'

BearCreature, rendered out of half a dozen Dog-Fellows and as hairy as a coconut, jerked his head forward, blinking apathetically. His long lower teeth poked out of his mouth. His powerful arms continued to hang slack.

'Who says?' he muttered.

'It is me – DogFellow,' and DogFellow raised himself, knocking loose a stone. BearCreature took a step backward.

'I want water.'

'If you are thirsty, then you must drink. I was only waiting here, for you.' DogFellow pointed at the nearest trough. *BearCreature, wary, mumbling words that were not words but fractured syllables mated to mere noise, went past and began to guzzle. DogFellow was appalled to see the want of ceremony, the free use of the tongue and lips.*

'You should not –' he began to say, but the noise of slurping overwhelmed everything else, even the bubble and swish of the water that overflowed from the troughs into the channel by their feet. When he brought his chin up silver drops dripped off BearCreature's beard and rained back on to the surface of the pool. He lifted and lowered his face three times, to drink only and not to wash. DogFellow saw this, and also the way his big hands (bigger than the Master's even, though infinitely more coarse) were caked with mud, and the nails all jagged.

'Where is your cup, friend?' asked DogFellow.

BearCreature wiped his mouth with the back of his forearm.

'Gone off somewhere,' he said, coming forward.

'No, don't leave, not yet,' said DogFellow, guessing BearCreature's intent. 'I have important news.'

BearCreature waved him away with an impatient gesture.

'Wait: you must listen.'

'No must.'

'Yes . . .'

DogFellow's own hand was upraised. If he were to set it against BearCreature, the flat of the palm would rest a little above the ragged waistline of the trousers he had on.

'The Master,' DogFellow said quickly. 'He has sent me.'

BearCreature did not flinch, as he properly ought to, but nor did he try to shove past.

'He sent me to talk to you,' continued DogFellow. 'He knew you would be here.'

'What?'

'He could not come himself.'

'But the Master – the Master – the Master away . . .'

'Only for a while.'

'Oh,' said BearCreature.

With one of his dirty nails he scratched absently at his hairy cheek. In the morning sun his shadow lay like a black slab across the stony ground.

'I know that the Master is not pleased with what we have done,' began DogFellow. 'For a long time now the beast people have not gone to speak the words of the Law. You have not gone yourself.'

'I go,' said BearCreature defensively.

'Did you go this morning?'

BearCreature stopped scratching his cheek and began to scratch his chin.

'No,' he said. 'Not this day.'

'Or the day before? Or the day before that?'

'I go.'

'And who did you see there?'

'I do not know them. They run away.'

DogFellow mustered up a look of abject solemnity. He shook his head.

'Oh, my friend, we have all sinned against the Law of the Master, and because of this he came, and talked to me.'

BearCreature grunted again, plainly discomforted by what he was hearing. DogFellow talked some more, but he was vague, and BearCreature did not have wit enough to ask an awkward question. The Master, as name and presence, had grown dull to him till that moment.

'And so tomorrow,' said DogFellow, 'you will go to the meeting post and you will wait.'

'Is – is the Master to come?'

'I do not know,' said DogFellow. 'All I know is what he has already told me.'

'He says about BearCreature?'

'Yes he does. He talked much of you and of the others.'

'His voice is loud?'

'At first yes,' said DogFellow. 'But he loves more than he hates. You remember that.'

'The hand – which hand?'

'This hand,' said DogFellow, and he held up the hand which strikes. 'But then, this hand.'

He reached out and touched BearCreature's dense forearm, brushing against the hair which grew there.

'You remember that too,' he said.

'Yes.'

'Then go tomorrow, as we used to.'

BearCreature looked as if he had another question, but then, with a shake of his head, he started to leave.

'Tell everyone you see,' said DogFellow to the wall of his retreating back.

'Everyone,' echoed BearCreature.

And he was gone, up the path. For the next hour DogFellow waited and he saw two more beast people; another hour and three came by. They did not turn up in groups but one by one, and all were as startled and as vaguely perturbed as BearCreature had been. DogFellow was always sure to let them drink first, and in this way he learned how all had foregone the use of the cup. He said nothing but added it to the list he had made in his head of things he would address at dawn the next day. Above all else, however, ought to be the business that occupied him from moment to moment, the great crime that had driven him there. And what if either of them should appear, wanting to dirty the water by washing in it, or wet their panting mouths? The notion set DogFellow's heart tripping every time he heard a footfall coming through the bushes. Yet he did not hide, because he was infused with the spirit of the Master, and from this courage flowed.

'Let them,' he said to himself. 'Let them come.'

However, they did not show their hated faces: there were only others, in their different shapes and sizes, their ancient clothes rotting on their bodies, their cups lost, their remembrance dull. He did not berate them. He simply repeated what he had told BearCreature, and every beast person thereafter.

'But he has gone away,' they said, with tongues half unstrung, paddling against the hard curves of every word.

DogFellow shook his head.

'He is near,' he said, again and again. 'He is near.'

Fourteen

DogFellow suddenly hears him howling, howling, like a
wolf or some equally savage creature. The others hear too,
as they mill about in the shadow of the House of Food,
ready for their midday mash. Sounds of anguish drifting
up out of the hidden chambers of the Master's compound
are, inevitably, nothing new. Every ear, irrespective of its
size and shape, has acquired a kind of filter, able to strain
out disagreeable noise. The beast people can eat and talk
in a seeming mood of tranquillity, as cows in a field will
eat. Indeed, the day before there was a ship, a steamer,
with an iron smokestack, moored out beyond the reef, off
the south-eastern end of the island, and they all left
their tasks to hide in the forest, while the supply boat went
back and forth, bearing boxes of supplies and cages in
which life fretted and snarled. The island ought to expect
a fresh round of cries to begin within a few hours. But the
noise they do hear – this noise, so different and so disagreeable – casts a pall over their patient waiting in the
dinner queue.

'What can be wrong?' asks Lemura.

'It is the other Master,' says another, rubbing her flat dish across her chest.

'No, no,' chips in Handy, three or four places behind. 'It is bad to speak that. Don't you know? There is no other Master.'

'Why do you say such things?' demands Fantine, looking over her shoulder.

'I don't say it,' mutters Handy. 'It is DogFellow – he told me.'

They all look across to where DogFellow squats, his steaming grub balanced on his knees. Their questions cease. That he still will come and sit thus, with his plate and his spoon, is a source of mild amazement, and they jealously cling to it, as proof of his ultimate failure; he has not moved beyond them, not yet. Fantine, always the boldest, speaks.

'Hey, DogFellow: why does the Master who is not a Master make such a sound? Is he going to die?'

DogFellow, who has taken to blowing on his food, as if he were at the dining table, looks up at her.

'No,' he says.

'Why then?'

'Does he have a sickness?' asks Handy.

'I do not know what he has got,' replies DogFellow. 'I have not seen him for a long time.'

'Why did he not go with the ship that came and went away?' asks Fantine.

'Because,' says DogFellow, giving renewed attention to his food.

'Why, DogFellow?'

'He could not.'

'The Master who is not a Master helps our own true proper Master,' offers Handy to any that will listen. 'He holds a little stick and makes marks in a paper book up and down like this.'

He waggles his crooked finger in imitation. In the distance the howling, that has been in abeyance for most of the previous few minutes, resumes again.

'I wish he would stop,' says Hector. And, though he does not say so, DogFellow wishes it too, with a true passion. He has been close enough to the compound to hear the language that intersperses the cries, the words that meld with strangulated yells. There are curses and threats and phrases that DogFellow knows along with those which he does not, yet he can guess, and all seems terrible.

'The Master who is not a Master seems very angry,' observes Fantine, helping herself from the cooking pot. 'Why is that, DogFellow?'

She wants him to yield up some titbit, but he can see through her language and is on his guard.

'His business is not my business,' he says, pronouncing the word by accentuating all three syllables. 'And it is not yours either.'

She gives a mock hiss, her tongue against her teeth, irritated rather than afraid.

'Why do you eat with us?' she suddenly exclaims. 'Surely you can do better if you beg for scraps at your Master's table?'

'He is Master to us all,' answers DogFellow, his tone quickening in tandem with the prickling of his nape. She sniffs and turns about, leaving him to eat the last of his meal. The backwash of anger destroys his appetite. He thinks how much he hates her, tells himself that this is what burns him, but turning this way and that in the forest of emotions he soon loses his way.

Only as dinner approaches does the doctor finally see fit to visit the stone room and its occupant.

'Are you awake?' he asks, because for several hours now there has been no sound at all from within.

'I'm going to kill you,' is the reply, rising out of the darkness, which reeks of excrement.

'I would ask you to refrain from speaking in that manner.'

'What have you done to me?'

'It was for your own benefit.'

'What was it you gave me?'

'A chemical agent. Nothing that could cause any permanent damage. I use it on occasion in my surgery.'

'An animal drug? O my God – O Jesus – Jesus . . .'

From out of the dark there comes the sudden sound of thrashing, as Henderson twists this way and that.

'What – what have you done to me? You've cut me, haven't you – you've been and cut me with your knives!'

'Don't be absurd. You were only put to sleep to save any bother. It was convenient to have you sedated; that is all.'

'Bastard! You disgusting bastard – you –'

'Mind your language, Mr Henderson. I'll not have needless cursing on this island.'

There is a sob and the movement stops. It is early evening and the sun is already in its embers, making it impossible to determine where Henderson is lying. The Master clicks his fingers and DogFellow hauls up the oil lamp he's dragged from the house. The Master takes it and turns up the wick. The spear of flame broadens, casting a faint cloud of yellowish light over the floor and walls of the stone house.

'The ship came, didn't it?' asks Henderson.

His face, grimacing at the loss of darkness, is uncovered in the near corner.

'Yes,' he is told, matter-of-factly, 'but that was yesterday.'

'What?'

'You've been here for nearly forty-eight hours. Captain van Toch has been and gone.'

Henderson does not reply for a few moments, and when he finally speaks it is evident even to DogFellow that he has started to cry.

'You can't do this,' he says. 'You can't keep me here –'

'Your very presence demonstrates the contrary,' says the Master, stooping to go closer.

He lets the lamp pass over the contour of Henderson's shoulder, hip and leg. He wrinkles his nose at the foul odour.

'They're going to be coming. They'll be here soon. People know where I am.'

'Nobody knows and nobody cares.' He takes Henderson's pulse. Henderson makes no attempt to resist.

'I have a family. I have a mother, father, two brothers, a fiancée. I've got colleagues, friends. I have a whole life back there. I cannot be allowed to just disappear. Everyone will be wondering about me –'

'We all have histories, Mr Henderson. Those connections we are born with, or accumulate. What you will find is how very fragile and how temporary these are.'

'I am not your prisoner –'

'I think you'll find you are. But only for a little while. It was a necessary measure. I knew you would agitate to try to get on board whatever vessel happened to stop by.'

'I could have gone.'

'Impossible.'

'Why?'

'You can't be expected to take passage on a ship like the one that visited –'

'It brought me here!'

'I won't hear of it. There are absolutely no conveniences for travel. Besides, I have grave reservations about the moral character of van Toch. I understand he is a fornicator. His personal hygiene is certainly abysmal. Now, turn this way. Try to look into the light.'

'Whether I come or go should be my decision.'

'Your pupils are still dilated.'

'Don't touch me!'

'You mustn't struggle.'

'You'd better let me go.'

'That is hardly reasonable. We have unfinished business.'

'Oh Lord, give me strength.'

'Surely you recognize your obligations –'

'There are no obligations!'

The Master tuts.

'You act dishonourably. We have an agreement. Your work is only half done. Do you really think I would let you loose, with my life story, my testament, the summation of all I have striven towards, crammed in your hand luggage, unfinished and unrevised? Would Galileo have allowed it? Would Newton?'

'I can't do any more.'

'Nonsense.'

'Every time I write something you put your pencil through it.'

'Because you aren't expressing events clearly, as they happened. Good God, is it so difficult?'

'Difficult? It's impossible.'

'Defeatist humbug.'

'Then do it your damn self.'

'No. You're here now. We've made a start. We have to persevere. You will bend to it. You will learn.'

'If you don't let me go – if you don't let me go at once – I swear – I – I won't be responsible for my actions, for what I will do.'

This is delivered with difficulty, as if Henderson is being suffocated by the weight of anger and frustration that bears down on him.

'Shush now,' mutters the Master. 'Everything will work

out for the best. If you apply yourself, then in a very few months the text will be finished, and I'll arrange your passage home. Hmmm: you seem to be running a fever . . .'

As the doctor brings his hand across the American's illuminated face, ready to press his palm against the sweat-stippled forehead, Henderson lunges. His teeth catch the web of skin that lies at the interstice between the thumb and index finger. The Master does not cry out, even as Henderson bites as hard as he can. Instead he grips the other man's nose and begins to squeeze, applying simultaneous pressure in forcing back the head. For a few moments some sort of deadly silence descends, a fit backcloth for this battle of endurance. There can be no real contest, since one is bound hand and foot while the other is free and could, if pressed by dire necessity, resort to a variety of tricks and stratagems. But DogFellow, the obvious ally, skulks to the rear, and the Master eschews even the most rudimentary strategy of punching the American in his purpling face.

In a short while it ends. With a tremendous sob Henderson relinquishes his bite and the life goes out of him. The Master inspects the torn skin and rising welt of blood.

'There was really no call for that,' he says. 'Fortunately being bitten on the hand is a risk I have inured myself to. Under ordinary circumstances, if you were not as you are, I would have no choice right now than to bring your life to an abrupt conclusion. But I am mindful of your obligations, as I have explained –'

There is a pause while a voluminous handkerchief is

pulled out of his pocket and set to his wound '– and I am determined that you will hold to it. If you prove yourself then you may be assured that soon enough – in six months or a year from now – we shall be able to come to a happy conclusion.'

Henderson will not reply. The only sound he makes comes from his laboured breathing.

'You will remain here to consider what I have suggested. I insist that you calm down. The drug is making you yield yourself to some approximation of a female passion, and that won't do. Control these silly fits, and when you reflect on what I've said I am quite sure you will be able to see things from a firm and reasoned perspective. Another twelve hours ought to assist the process.'

'No. I don't want to be left,' says Henderson.

'Till tomorrow,' says the Master.

'At least loosen the ties around my legs.'

The Master considers, then says, 'Very well.'

While he is about the business Henderson says, 'I'm terribly thirsty.'

The Master gives the nod to DogFellow, who goes and brings back a pannikin filled to the brim. He can see how Henderson has been pulled up off his side, and listens to what the Master is saying to him. He accepts water from the Master's hand, gulping it hard, so that it dribbles down over his chin. As soon as this is done the Master turns to leave.

'You'll be back first thing?' Henderson calls out pitifully.

'Yes,' he is told, and so he is left, to spend the night, and reflect on the nature of the pact he is mired in.

But in the morning, when DogFellow arrives, with coconut milk and breadfruit, Henderson has already gone.

Fifteen

He stares at the puddle of light which has somehow squeezed under the far wall. Save for this, and two almost symmetrical heaps of dirt, the chamber is empty. It takes him a short while to understand that this is more than a curious and unexpected phenomenon, and that the Master who is not nor ever was a Master has somehow slipped his bonds, excavated a tunnel and gone away.

He calls out as he runs back through the gate towards the house. The doctor, standing before his work bench, dabbing iodine on his own hand, receives the news. At once, without rolling down his shirtsleeve, he follows DogFellow to the scene. Viewed from the back of the stone house the hole seems scarce large enough to admit a rabbit, though a single bloody palm print high up on the grey pumice shows that Henderson did pass this way.

'Do you know anything about it?' he demands, turning his big angry face on DogFellow. Without waiting for an answer he kicks at the loose earth and then goes to scan the ground, for any tangible proof that Henderson is still about, cowering in the vicinity, though it is more than evident that he has disappeared into the lusty herbage which begins yards from the rear of the settlement and lies like a blanket over the rest of the island.

'Henderson!' he shouts, before the wall of green. 'You liar! Hear me? You – are – a – liar! Do you think you can run away and forget your debts? You promised me!'

It is almost too much for him. Choking, he stumbles, coughing and spluttering and almost vomiting up his breakfast. DogFellow draws near but is waved away.

With his uninjured hand the Master unbuttons the neck of his shirt, wheezing in rage. It is several minutes before he straightens himself and strides back towards DogFellow. The anger is still there, but it has been contained and lies like a hornet under glass, with only the faintest audible vibration catching the ear. DogFellow, of course, senses it and quails.

'Very well, we'll let him run,' says the Master, still striding. 'After all, where is he going to go? If he tries to build a raft it will go to pieces on the reef. Either that or the sharks will get him. But he won't do that. He is weak. He hasn't an ounce of resourcefulness in his body, the miserable cur. Let him go, let him go. Perhaps he thinks he can hide out somewhere and wait for the next ship? Well, we'll see how long he lasts before he starves. Let him go; yes, that's the way –'

At the door to the house he stops. He seems faintly surprised that DogFellow is still there, at his heel.

'Go and fill in that hole,' he says, before returning to his interrupted work.

*

Two days later – no more than that – and the rumour goes about that some observant nose has caught the odour of woodsmoke snaking across the island. A week goes by and the smell is found again, and this time, from the slopes that rise up above the compound, it is possible to look east and see a vertical streak of grey, rising up and up before catching on the wind and disappearing.

'It is the Master who is no longer a Master,' they whisper. 'It is him, the one with the paper book and the stick that goes up and down, the one who cried out –'

And they consider asking DogFellow for an explanation, and DogFellow considers going to the Master, but the Master – omniscient, omnipotent – has the matter in hand, and soon he himself is studying the smoke plume through his pocket telescope.

'Must be trying to attract a ship,' he observes. 'Or cooking something. Or perhaps he's set himself alight.' Then he says, 'Are you there, or am I talking to myself?'

'I am here, Master,' replies DogFellow.

'I want you to go over and find out what he's up to.'

'Master?' The tone is more than a little querulous.

The doctor lowers his eyepiece and glares.

'Do I have to repeat myself?'

DogFellow, shocked by his own temerity, stares at the ground.

'You will go over there and find out what you can. Just make sure he doesn't spot you. Then you come straight back and tell me. Let me know exactly how he is, what he's up to. Is that plain enough or do I have to drub it into that thick head of yours?'

'Yes, Master. But the washing –'

'Confound the washing! Let Handy do it! Enough! Go, get out of my sight and no dawdling!'

Muttering darkly, he resumes his study of the sky.

Henderson did not run deep into the heart of the woods, preferring to skirt the densest vegetation and steepest ground, so that his path took him across the lobe of ash and rock that constitutes the southernmost part of the island. This much is evident to DogFellow as he traces his way along a ghostly track, perhaps made by goats (long since flushed out and shot) or perhaps by the island's first unknown inhabitants, ages ago.

The sprinkle of blood he detects on a tree trunk and the lingering stink of man-piss ten yards on tells him that Henderson took this route for sure, and when DogFellow discovers a sudden break in the canopy and spies the smoke column, finger-thick rather than running like a crack up the sky, he understands that he has drawn near.

All too mindful of the Master's stern words he is careful to keep to cover, and rather than pursue the path as it meanders its way back down to the beach he bears to the north-east, struggling through ferns as tall as himself until he is up on a thickly vegetated headland and able to look down on to rocks and sand. He is close enough now to hear the crackle and pop of dead palm leaves and other woody scraps set in a pyramid above the winking light of the fire.

On this side of the island the reef lies much further out, and the white breakers seem like a smudge, spoiling the fusion of sea and sky. The lagoon itself becomes an immensity, lying flat and still. DogFellow notices a line of sticks, poking up in a row a little way out: he considers that this must be Henderson's attempt at a fish trap. He also can see a cave – an irregular split in the basalt – which, by virtue of the scraps and muck heaped outside, must constitute Henderson's shelter. There is at that moment no sign of the man himself.

Ah, thinks DogFellow: what if he is asleep? What if – what if he is dead?

DogFellow scratches his ribs in sudden perplexity. A greater itch has hold of him, and despite the risk he begins to creep forward, going on all fours to avoid slipping.

When nearly level with the beach he huddles against a palm trunk and once more tries to find sign of movement. But there is none, and though another hour goes by, it seems as if Henderson has truly disappeared. He remembers all that the American told him, of countries far away full of strange things: of the place called Unitedstates, which is the same as Paris, which means civilization. What if Henderson has already gone back there? Perhaps, at that moment he is thinking of DogFellow, even as DogFellow is thinking of him –

But no, it cannot be. Even with half his face pressed to the solid mass of a tree, his ear can catch the far-out cannonade of waves striking against the coral that encircles the only world in existence. If Henderson ever dared to build a raft and tried to sail away, he died in the attempt, and the sharks ate him.

Then DogFellow sees how high the fuel upon the fire

has been heaped, and reasons that this must be the consequence of recent effort. So, if there were a raft, he would still be able to spy it, out on the back of the ocean. But there is nothing. Therefore, Henderson must be near. In reflex to this, DogFellow lowers himself, so that his belly is against the sandy dirt. Behind him a thorn bush gives some measure of protection. He watches the mouth of the cave and waits.

Time passes. If only DogFellow could pass too, out beyond himself, becoming a distant whitecap rolling on the Pacific, or else a twig barely trembling in the slight breeze. Yet his thoughts are dense and smoky, like the grey murk seeping off the blackened palm branches, and he looks up only to notice how the sun is crossing the sky.

What can he tell the Master? That Henderson lives, and waits for some kind of deliverance, some ending. He must be asleep. It would be a bold thing to go and look, but DogFellow holds back and at last, as afternoon passes into evening, he gets up and begins to climb up the way he came.

Sixteen

By the time he reaches level ground again the shadows cast
by the trees are lengthening. He moves noisily through the
ferns, sometimes becoming submerged entirely, and in
the deepening gloom he finds the path.

But DogFellow has not gone far when he experiences
the disconcerting sensation of no longer being alone. To
begin with there is only a distant sound, like the wind in
the trees setting leaf against leaf, and he gives it no attention; and then, behind him, quite suddenly, comes the
noise of something heavy tumbling into a mass of friable
twigs, and the confusion lasts for several long moments.

Alarmed, he picks up his pace: the path he moves along
is not straight and though he could try and look over his
shoulder he can see only trees, set like a wall across the way
he has travelled. From beyond this, again, he detects something new – the wheeze of hoarse breathing – to set beside
the sudden revived racket of snapping and swishing.

DogFellow, frightened now, begins to run as best he
can, with the legs he has been gifted: each accelerated step

sends his upper body slewing left and right, and for fear of losing his balance he keeps his arms stiff and half raised. Once, his foot cracks hard into the snaky root of some looming tree and he is cast off balance, ending on his back, his ribcage swelling and shrinking in tandem with the exertion of his lungs and poor labouring heart, but he is somehow up and running again even as his pursuer treads on the place where he's been. Down a slope full of stones he goes and stumbles a second time, except that now he saves himself by using his hands and scrambles on.

Behind him the other comes on in close pursuit, unrelenting even in the face of whipping branches and a path that is no longer a path but a break between bushes and tree columns. DogFellow somehow sees the dense angularity of a jutting bough and by suddenly making himself low is able to get beneath and clear with only a scraped back to show for it, while the one who pursues goes full tilt into the obstruction, but still DogFellow does not slow his momentum, indeed cannot slow the furious tempo of his crooked legs as the already steep slope steepens further and then, in another few paces, drops away altogether. Something rips at DogFellow's face and he feels himself turn, turn, before being swallowed by a greater darkness, full of the noise of snapping twigs and agitated leaves. The breath goes out of him entirely and he is thrown first forwards and then back until a brilliant light sparks in his head and he sees the sun rising over the sea, more dazzling than he has ever witnessed. Then it is suddenly dark again and he has returned to the flat, hard, uncomfortable earth.

He knows he is hurt, and half afraid and half giddy he

tries to get up, only to feel the stab and rake of the bush he has landed in pull at his back and shoulders. So he crawls, although awkwardly, because of the sickening deadness that has taken hold of his right arm.

He finds himself on the sand again. Across the dusky plane of the beach is the Pacific, not effulgent as in his vision but inky beneath a night sky. After a while he tries to stand, and now the agony of his right arm is matched by a dreadful pain in his side. When with his good hand he rubs at his face there is the wetness of blood on his fingers. Unthinking, he licks at it and whimpers to himself. He finds he can walk, though his legs are unsteady.

Looking back, he is just able to make out the rise down which he has tumbled. Is it thirty, forty paces high? At the very top the forest is static, running like a black crest in either direction, as far as he can see. After a few dazed moments he realizes that he has in fact emerged much closer to the compound than would have been the case if he had kept to the path. Ahead he can make out the cluster of palm trees that the beast people are wont to shelter among during the hot afternoons.

Slowly he skirts the grove, bearing westwards. He glances nervously towards the stand of trees as he goes and at that moment seems to see how one shadow runs contrary to the fixed mass of fuzzy-headed darkness. It disappears in the next eye blink. The vague unreality of the chase culminating in the fall has elicited a like daze in DogFellow's mind, yet now with the burn of his injuries rising and the familiar vista of sea and beach about him he feels real fear jerking at his tender belly. He is not fool enough to stop and peer further into the night, nor does he break out of his awkward hobble. Beyond the next little jut of land he knows he will see the distant glimmer of lamplight that marks the Master's house.

Trying to think only of this he grinds his teeth together and yet, greater than all his physical agony, is the rising awareness of movement at his back, passing through the grove and then breaking cover. DogFellow chokes on the sudden terror that nearly overwhelms him, wishing he had a stick, a stone, anything. He must once more let his legs carry him forward, slogging across the level, with the whisper of the ocean in contrast to his own ragged gasps and the sound of something else thud-thudding through the sand a dozen – ten – eight yards behind. This time there are no low boughs to lend mute assistance, and the ground does not accelerate his passage: he is utterly exposed as he takes the narrow corridor of sand that funnels out on to the Master's beach, with the compound in the distance and a square of light pressed on to its sooty flank. It is on this point that DogFellow fixes all hope as he limps and stumbles forward, choking on the night air, which lies in his throat like a clot of gauze. The deadly burn of his arm and ribs has now been ousted by the agony in his lungs, as the light ahead seems to flicker and then smear itself across the darkness, becoming a phosphorescent squiggle. And it is too late, it is all too late, for the other is upon him, catching at the hem of his flapping shirt, pulling Dog-Fellow to a violent halt and a still more violent end.

He cries out, putting all that remains to him into a single howl of 'Master!' before slipping forward amid a nauseating confusion of sand and black sky and the sob of his own bitter breath.

The light he has been running towards has vanished and in its place burns a single point of redness, glowering at him as he grovels in pain and terror, before swooping down, to scald out his eyes and burn him to a puddle of tar. He squeals and squirms, feeling his upper lip riding up over his teeth in a desperate grimace.

'What on earth are you doing?'

For an instant DogFellow continues to feel that his own life is forfeit, his jangling brain incapable of making sense of the words that come to him out of the dark above his head. Then, powerfully, mysteriously, he feels the strong hands grasp at his shoulders and shake the panic from him.

The Master, the lit cigar still clenched between his teeth, is uttering gruff words of command, which form a rock that DogFellow can cling to. After a while he is sensible enough to blink up through tear-stained eyes and mutter his gratitude. The Master tosses his postprandial smoke aside and drags DogFellow to his feet.

'Get up,' he shouts, 'and stop snivelling. I can't understand a word you're saying.'

'Behind me Master – he comes –'

DogFellow points back the way he fled, back towards the sibilant ocean.

'Who? Henderson? He chased you?'

With a growl he lets DogFellow fall back on to his rump while he runs in the direction implied, his big body and white suit flashing like a ghost in the starlight. DogFellow, alone once more, trembles pathetically. Fear and relief and humiliation claim him. He sits and waits, unable to move; when the Master reappears he cannot resist bowing his head and raising up his shoulders in abject submission. The Master is too irate to notice.

'You do realize that I had to serve myself at dinner tonight, while you were outside running about the island like an idiot?'

DogFellow mumbles nothing in reply.

'You say he chased you? You chased yourself, you dunce.'

'By the trees . . .'

'The only footprints I can find are yours. There's not a trace of anyone else. And stand up while I'm talking to you.'

DogFellow obeys but cannot stifle a yelp of pain.

'Good God: look at you.'

DogFellow whimpers and wipes his nose with the back of his forearm. The blood has begun to dry on the side of his face. The pain in his ribs has swollen into an unbearable agony.

'Did you find out where he is?'

DogFellow nods.

'Did you see him?'

He shakes his head. There are other questions which he tries to answer, despite the rising tide of mortal sickness that creeps over him, filling his ears with a rushing noise like the rush of water from the pump, so that the voice he hears becomes fainter and still fainter.

'And he keeps the fire burning as a beacon?' the Master asks, expecting a useful answer. But all he gets is Dog-Fellow tumbling forwards to lie in a dead faint by his boots.

Far away, close to the point where sea and sky rested belly to belly, something moved, processing from right to left. Of course, it might only be a trick of the light, but a quick rub of the eyes failed to dispel its existence. There was something for definite, something that hovered, neither of the air nor of the water. His mouth was as dry as the dirt underfoot and his body shook. Where were they, those wretched others, that they were not witnessing this fulfilment of everything he had sworn would happen?

Before dawn he had come to the assembly field, and in his mind's eye, his mind's ear, he could almost rekindle the tramp-tramp of feet all around, and the mood of anxious expectation, waiting for the flicker of light against the window, so he was more than distressed to find he was by himself when the sun finally lit up the world. Now however – now who would be sorry?

Of course, he had done all he could among the beast people, beginning with the long hours he'd spent up by the water trough, and later out in the woods, discovering those clearings and semi-arboreal nests that had, it appeared, become the refuge and centre of island life. They were there, in the trees, behind the trunks, masked by branches, yet though he called out, specifying names (guessing at who might be who) none replied. So he had had to content himself with roaming about, looking for signs, finding proof inadvertently, once when he trod in excrement and later when a coconut dropped from out of a banyan tree perilously close to his head. As he went he told whoever might be listening the story (very familiar already) of how the time for disorder had ended, and that they were all of them soon to be tried by the Master. He had said how the Master not gone away at all – no, no; he was merely hidden, in a secret place, the better to study the ways of all his children, and they must prepare to have him come back, and pass judgement. They would look up to see again that terrible brow, those raised hands, the one to caress, the other, the other . . .

Back on the beach, scrutinizing the horizon, DogFellow thought of those hands and tried, despite the haze and the ache of his eyes, to perceive if either was extended in some gargantuan gesture across the blue lens of the Pacific.

Master, Master, spare me –

Let it be the good hand , he prayed, the right hand. Yet what if it was instead the left?

Master, Master, it was not I –

He, DogFellow, could not be the worst of them. It was impossible to imagine it, not when there were others who lapped with the tongue and lived in the forest and let their clothes lie next to their skin in stinking rags. And, above all, not while Hector and Fantine lived on, mired in the filth of their own making.

Let them be taken and crushed for their betrayal. Let them be cut again and again and again –

The distant figure seemed to coalesce, gathering in substance, even though it appeared no closer. In contrast, down below, the sea lost definition, breaking up into a field of luminous hexagonals which winked in and out of existence. It was too much. His vision faded, and his eyes closed up, the lids bunched together in a sudden spasm –

Where were they, those others who could be his eyes right now, telling him of the things he already saw inside his heart? Yet – yet it was better to be alone. Yes! He would be the one to bound down through the surf and welcome the Master. He could explain everything. The others did not know. The others were fools – or worse.

Master, Master, help me –

As if in answer – as if even from far across the sea He could hear, and insinuate soothing ophthalmic drops on to each overburdened cornea – the pain passed, and Dog-Fellow might again bear to look out and find his black point. There it was, absolutely distinct in its physical substance yet, by dint of the way it hung between sea and sky, more than physical. If he looked hard enough could he make out the face? He tried, and for a moment was transported to imagine that there was a face, with the white hair swept back and the broad brow, but this had gone in an instant.

Watching and waiting, he was not conscious of time passing by although the sea withdrew to is furthest point *and started to beat back up the beach again. The heat of the afternoon sun was kept off by a cooling seaborne wind, and even if he should be scorched, what was that in exchange for the honour of seeing the Master, aloof and majestic and unwilling as yet to venture ashore?*

Because we do not deserve it.

DogFellow told this to the world, as afternoon yielded to evening and the point he had regarded finally lost its presence.

We do not deserve it and so he still waits.

Somehow this explanation – which occurred quite spontaneously – was enough to give comfort. He turned, to go back inland, and fell flat on his face. Perhaps this was how it must be: DogFellow summoned to the Master rather than the other way around. But no. He fell because his body had been punished enough and wanted only a little respite. He could feel the warm sand against his cheek and the gritty texture on his lips. Why, though, were his feet in front of his face? Curious rather than anxious he lifted his head a fraction and saw not just feet (more naked and malformed, in truth, than his own) but ankles and the implication of a separate and distinctive body.

'Leave me,' he said.

The other stooped, the feet levering forward and the knees bobbing low.

'What do you do here?'

He was being asked a question. He struggled to keep the black void that wanted to eat up his consciousness at bay.

'You should have been here, earlier,' DogFellow began.

'No come. Bad place.'

'You – you're the bad place. Inside your heart.'

He tried to look up, but the beast was all murk, with the constancy of a flickering shadow.

'The Master,' he continued, 'I saw him here today. He is so near he will be able to come when he likes. Tonight perhaps . . . not here, but on the other side of the island. He has another house –'

Ideas and explanations he had never had before seemed to be occurring without the slightest effort on his part.

'Can't you understand what I'm telling you? Why don't you answer?'

'Master not come,' said the other at last.

'I saw him!'

'Gone forever. You saw him then, not now. Master is dead.'

'Liar!'

He would have struck his fist into the sand but was too weak.

'You know, DogFellow. You clever: better than any other. You know –'

'I know?'

'Master gone – door locked –'

DogFellow swiped with his hand, missed, and tried to pull himself up.

'Sleep and forget,' said the other.

'Hector, is that you?'

'Forget,' said the voice.

'BlueBob?'

There was no reply.

'Jasper? Ebor? L-Lucky?'

He went on while he could, while he thought the other might still be listening, crying out names that had finally lost whatever purchase they'd ever had upon the world – now only husks, or rags, fallen away from the things they'd once contained. It did no good. The other had disappeared. His voice sank to a whisper, then guttered, threatening to go out altogether. He closed his sandy lips and swallowed, coaxing a little spit down his dry throat. He understood how it must be.

He was alone now: alone.

Seventeen

'You want to eat?' asks Handy.

DogFellow opens one eye. There is a bowl of food passing to and fro by his nose: a congealed slop of yam and mashed coconut. He turns his head towards the far wall of the infirmary. He has watched that wall for days, slipping in and out of fever. He'd never have thought it, but he has grown used to lying in this place. He hears Handy snort, and say 'Fair enough. Never mind. If you do not want this good scoff I can think of a chap who does.'

Sticking in a wooden spoon Handy gives the bowl a quick stir.

'Plenty good food I bring here,' he declares. 'Two bowls a day and always you don't want. Fair enough, never mind I say. But the Master, he will not be so easy with you when he asks and I tell him. Always tell the truth, never lie. Perhaps tonight he asks, yes, tonight he will want to know, when I give him his own dinner.'

There is a pause, then DogFellow, turning back, asks, 'What dinner?'

'So, ha-ha, you waked after all,' says Handy, before shovelling a loaded spoon into his mouth.

'What Master's dinner?' repeats DogFellow.

'Our Master, nitwit!'

The words are muffled, and accompanied by a spray of coconut flecks.

'*You* take it to him?'

'Mmmm-hmmm.'

Handy licks the back of the spoon with his stumpy tongue.

'No, no,' says DogFellow, almost to himself. 'You don't do that. It is not right –'

He tries to sit up and finds he can't, because the bandages are wrapped too tightly against his ribs.

'You got to stay quiet and not go walking any place,' explains Handy. 'You nearly killed dead with sickness.'

'But dinner – that's *my* job –'

'Mine now,' says Handy, cramming in another spoonful. Perhaps it is because of the bandages that DogFellow finds it increasingly difficult to breathe.

'You been sick,' Handy says. 'Deadly sick, three or four days together. Sick in your sleep, shouting this and that. This thing you say, this word –'

Handy wrinkles his hairy nose, trying for a second or two to remember, before forgetting what it is he's supposed to be thinking about.

'Good job you got a friend like me!' he continues, cheerfully. 'I come to help you, DogFellow.'

Again the bowl, half empty, is pushed into DogFellow's face.

'Take it away.'

Handy shrugs and eats. After he has finished, he says, 'Yes, it is me and Hector that makes nice food for the Master. And in the day Hector goes and carries about the bottles and then cleans the sharp, shiny knives . . .'

DogFellow slowly lifts his good left arm – the other, encased in plaster, lies like a stone limb alongside him – and scratches an itch on his face.

'But now . . . now I am well again,' he says. 'I can do whatever is wanted.'

'No,' says Handy, pressing his palm gently against Dog-Fellow's bare leg. 'You sleep, old chap. I tell the others, I tell them "Ah, it goes bad with poor DogFellow these days. He is old and tired."'

'I'm no different from you!' DogFellow is hurt beyond measure by what is being suggested. 'The Master, he made us at the same time, almost –'

'But not younger than Hector. He comes later. Ah, he has strength! I have seen him carry the Master's iron stick as if it were the same as this.'

And Handy very carefully balances the spoon across his outstretched index finger, which is thin and warped and ugly.

'What?' DogFellow mutters. 'He has done that?'

'Oh yes,' says Handy, as if he had borne witness to something miraculous. 'And he had the bag too – you know, the bag that goes clink-clink, that feeds the iron stick.'

'When was all this?'

'Hmm?'

'When – when – when did it happen –'

'Ah – it was . . . mmm . . .'

In the obtuseness of his deliberations, and in the slow, almost imbecilic habit he has of holding his head deathly still while allowing his chin to droop, Handy makes the agitated DogFellow want to howl. But then, having some-how reckoned the intervening time, he says, 'Two days ago, when our Master went to jaw-jaw with the Master who is not a Master: you know who. They went a long way into the woods and stayed there, from breakfast to suppertime and we were afraid because Lemura said that the Master who is not a Master had played a trick and would make himself king over all the island and put us in cages, or kill us. But then our Master came back and we were glad; we shouted "Hurrah! Hurrah!", like that. And Hector was there, right behind . . .'

'Behind him?'

Handy nods.

There is much else in the way of tiresome opinion and useless gossip, which DogFellow, rocked into a sick kind of daze, cannot take in, although afterwards he picks over what he has learned with the same feverish worry his fingers bring to bear on the edge of the frayed blanket, tug-ging and twisting each thread in turn. He wants to believe that none of it is true. But when he finally drops into a doze he is subject over and over to scenes that cut into him like a knife.

Twice he tries to get out of bed, but is driven down by the dead weight of his right arm and the sharp hurt in his ribs, so in the end he must lie still and wait, wait through all the long night, with the frets and terrors that prey upon the thinking mind preying upon him. And it seems he has only just gained the benefit of oblivion when, with a rattle and a bang, Handy is back, bearing his breakfast bowl. DogFellow will refuse it. But there, bringing up the rear, is the Master.

He enters without speaking, without offering any sign of acknowledgement at all, and is immediately brisk and busy. First one of the other beds has its mattress turned, and then the window shutter is opened a few inches. Observing something run across the floor, he swoops and takes it up; it receives a moment's cursory attention before being allowed to fall back beneath his boot. Directly afterwards he seems lost in thought, setting his fingers to rub at his beard: perhaps it is the transience of all life that holds him; perhaps the mutability of reputation. All DogFellow knows is that long moments are dragging by, during which he himself is dying, not once but over and over again, because he sees in these actions the supreme loftiness the Master always brings to bear on the sick-room, and understands that he has passed beyond the pale and must now take his place in a wilderness populated by wretched creatures who possess nothing to show for themselves except their sick and sutured bodies. And sure enough, when he finally steps over to where DogFellow lies, there is no flicker of recognition, not in the eyes, not in the movement of the hands. These waft indifferently past DogFellow's face and settle on the wrappings about his torso. With a quick tug the fitness of the knot is tested. He evidently considers it sound enough, because then he reaches across to evaluate the plastered arm, lifting it slightly and roughly squeezing the shoulder joint.

'Need to keep it exercised or there'll be atrophy.'

These are his words, but spoken for his own benefit, not DogFellow's. That DogFellow should be privy to it is an accident of no greater moment than the fact that the floorboards squeak when the Master stands.

'Tomorrow,' he says. 'A little fresh air. A turn about the yard. You –'

He is addressing Handy, who quails and bows and seeks to contract himself into as small a space as possible without actually moving.

'– why are you still here?'

'Master . . .' says Handy in a strangulated whine and holds out the bowl he has, showing DogFellow's breakfast.

'Well, leave it for him. He's not a complete cripple. I don't like this loitering. You're a damned loiterer. Put down that food and get on with your chores.'

Handy bows, doing as he is told before scuttling away, passing like a shadow across the floor of the infirmary: a wooden floor, the better to be scrubbed and kept as clean as picked bone. Thus DogFellow and the Master find themselves by themselves, as they have been so many times in the past, when they inhabited what seemed a companionable silence, with books and pipe smoke and the tick-tock of the old timepiece. And the recollection of all this makes the love DogFellow bears seem like a boulder he has swallowed, threatening to crush his heart. He wants so much to be acknowledged that he wishes his arm would suppurate, rot and fall off, just for the blessing it would bring. But with a heedless flex of his big shoulders the Master has turned his back – has walked to the door – and is gone.

Eighteen

The beast man known as Jasper breaks away from the small work gang and comes towards him. Roll-call has just taken place. The Master berated his creation for its more than usual tardiness in tripping out the mantra all must live by, and then went indoors again. DogFellow, his arm now mended, waits for a while on the edge of the assembly ground, although he knows what will follow. The night before he learned he was to be requisitioned as a wood-gatherer. Now Jasper is talking to him.

'You come with us today,' he says. 'Before, you go and fetch a basket. You got to fill him up; you savvy?'

DogFellow does not reply and does not meet Jasper's gaze, which is steady and uncomplicated. Instead he pretends to study his feet, and the patch of earth between them.

'It is not so bad,' says Jasper, by way of consolation; then he gives up, and goes back to the others.

The sun has already sprung clear of the horizon when they start out, yet the air still possesses a residual coolness, and the sweet dusky smells of the night cling to it. There are four of them altogether, walking along the dirt track, between bushes fat with birdsong. Jasper goes a yard in front; Lucky and Hobbs follow, walking side by side. They are all of them physically larger than DogFellow, betraying their ancestries in different ways. Hobbs is so beset with muscle that there is scarcely room left for a tongue or brain. His back is enormously wide and connects to the rear of his head without bothering about the formality of a neck. DogFellow remembers when the Master made him, remembers the disappointment as the bold conception ran awry, and the hair's-breadth decision that meant life over death. DogFellow played his part in this. 'Well, boy?' he had been asked. 'What's it to be?' And he had given some sign – he is sure he did, though he cannot recall what – which had spared the hulking brute who moves ahead of him now, swinging his arms from side to side with such dumb insolence.

They reach the valley a while later, just as it is beginning to get hot. They have travelled to the north-east of the settlement, a little under a mile. The air is full of daytime forest smells, and underlying these – always and unchanging – there is the odour of the sea. If anything, the sound of the birds has grown louder.

They carry machetes, a gift of trust made a little more secure by the fact that the blades are dull. Each of them must load up their woven baskets with chopped sticks, sufficient to feed the fires of the kitchen and the wash hut. Without ceremony they begin. DogFellow goes off by himself, feeling ill with disgust. As he works he can hear Jasper and Lucky calling out to each other, throwing friendly insults or else speculating about the meal they might get later on. Once or twice they call out to him, and he makes out he is too absorbed in his task to hear. When they are stooped over he casts the occasional glance in their direction, thinking about how similar they look, with their strong straight legs and corded arms. Their faces are the same too – ugly monkey faces, scarcely marked by the Master's knife. He smirks sardonically when he sees how at midday they go and fetch a twelve-fingered hand of bananas to share among themselves. He shakes his head at his portion and carries on working all through the afternoon, though for every ten sticks he picks up nine are thrown down again, out of some scruple. Once he thinks he catches them looking at him – all three of them, as if sharing in some joke at his expense. He nearly goes over to demand what it is they find so amusing, but in the end he swallows his rising bile and gets on with accumulating wood.

At last Jasper says, 'We done now. Come on.' He has tied a rag about the span of his forehead, to soak up the perspiration, though the intense warmth of late afternoon is now passing. The others are quick to gather their few things and depart. Jasper spends a little while wiping down the blade of his machete with a fistful of coarse grass. He blows down its length and eyes it with a practised air. DogFellow, who has abandoned his task and sits disconsolately on an old tree stump, does not move and pretends not to watch.

Satisfied, Jasper sticks his tool in the rope that is

twisted and tied about his middle. He suddenly seems aware that DogFellow has not gone yet. He says, 'Hey, talking to you too.'

Away, at the mouth of the valley, staggering beneath the weight of their load, Lucky and Hobbs can be seen, one wide, one tall. They disappear out of sight.

'You deaf now, old chap?'

Jasper shows no asperity, yet he is impatient to be gone, thinking of dinner, his life's lodestar. He drags his basket after him and, reaching out, goes to pat at DogFellow's shoulder, perhaps to reassure himself that this is not some relapse, or a new malaise.

'What is it?'

'Don't touch me!' hisses DogFellow.

'Oh,' says Jasper, startled. He goes off a few paces, then turns about. 'Why you say that?' he asks.

'I don't want you near me,' says DogFellow. 'You or them.'

'What? Why you talk like that? You come along; dinner-time is nearly here –'

'Not hungry.'

'Come on! You work at a proper job now. You don't eat and *phht!*: you go thin and sick and you no good to me no more. You no good to no one. We back tomorrow all too soon, so clean your ears out and run along. I have heard it is a good dinner day today. If we are quick we will get extra.'

DogFellow does not react. It is as if he has gone stone deaf.

'Quick about it and take your basket too! Looks like that won't be heavy to carry home –'

DogFellow breaks his silence.

'Shut your stupid mouth,' he mutters.

Jasper, confused more than angry, blinks as if just slapped across the face.

'What you say?'

'I said – I said shut up!'

'Now listen DogFellow, you must not lay your bad words on me –'

'I will lay more than bad words on you if you do not leave me alone. Go on, get away. You make my insides rise up: ugh! Ugh!'

'You have such words for your own brother?'

'I am not your brother! How dare you say that! How dare you say "brother" to me, you – you dirty cockroach!'

DogFellow has leapt off his stump, trembling with rage, and now the two stand only a yard apart. Jasper is the larger by far, but something terrible in DogFellow's demeanour compels him to hold back.

'The apes in the trees may be brothers to you but I am not. No, not I! I am a man, a proper man, with civilization, and a hat and a cane and boots, while you –'

DogFellow cannot muster the words, such is the torrent of wrath and grief coursing through him, and his voice disintegrates into a whining snarl.

Jasper – appalled in his heart but held fast by an anger of his own, his dinner finally forgotten – slowly grasps what it is that has been consuming DogFellow, and makes his reply.

'Ah, so it is! You think you still better than best because the Master gave you a little stick to go up and down with?'

'Shut up, idiot! Shut up, bumpkin! Animal! You don't know what you're talking about!'

'Oh, DogFellow, DogFellow. There is no more of that. That stick goes up and down for Hector now. You belong with us these days. You and me – we're the same.'

'Never!'

'Look, look,' says Jasper, pointing to the dirty clothes they wear, stained with sweat and tree sap and flakes of wood. 'Same, same, same. All the same. Not in the Master's house now, old chap. It is in the fields, in the woods, with me and Lucky and all other beast peoples, over and over again, this day, tomorrow and then the next day after. Brothers, brothers –'

But DogFellow has already turned his back and started to stalk away, his face convulsed. He feels he will commit murder if he stays. It would be easy enough to snatch up a machete, or even a chunk of stone, and split Jasper's stupid head open, from crown to chin and then, afterwards, to dance in the puddle of his mashed-up brains –

He begins to walk down the valley, going fast, leaving Jasper and the baskets of kindling far behind himself. He then strikes east, towards the settlement, meaning to hide out in his hut, but nearing the fruit groves, he sees, in the middle distance, other beast people fussing about a wheelbarrow, and so he turns southwards, heading for the nearest patch of trees, and by the time he reaches the dusky shade his anger has cooled, leaving despair behind, as black and boundless as the igneous rock on which the island is founded. Despair and pity and tears are his, and afterwards the night and an empty belly.

But the very next day he can do nothing except return to the fringes of the forest, to pick up wood and cut off branches. The others do not speak to him, although once or twice they look his way, curious, not understanding.

Nineteen

It is half an hour before noon and the sun is fiercely hot, feeling tight about the head like an iron brace and burning the shoulders of anyone thoughtless enough to leave the shade. Thus it is that all the beast people are dozing beneath the trees, or else taking their rest where they can, in the fields or close by the House of Food. Only Dog-Fellow is up and active, wielding the brush with which he has been whitewashing rocks.

He perspires as well as he can and once or twice surrenders to a bout of panting, but then he gathers himself, doing up his mouth and blinking the sweat out of his eyes. He makes no effort to go and lie down. Throughout the morning he has been busy with his bucket, giving the boundary markers that section off the assembly ground their hundredth lick of paint. It was not to be his job – it had been allocated to some beast, who DogFellow had hardly noticed before – but a simple bribe was enough to change the work rota, and so the task passed his way. Already, after only a month, he understands how such things can be effected. For even half a dinner there are those who will happily conclude a swap.

It is not so much the nearness to his old abode that put DogFellow up to it. There is something strangely congenial in the action of making the dull powdery surface of each grey rock glisten with whiteness. He thinks of the bandages he has boiled and the clothes he has washed; the very special collars he has starched, and other things too – sacred to memory – which dazzle and half-blind him, just as the rocks do now, in all the glory of their transfigured livery. He works slowly and methodically and has only done one row, although it is an impeccable display. From time to time as he paints he glances up, watching the main gate of the compound. It is quiet today – no voice raised; no muffled screeching. At midday, a little before the dinner bell is sounded, a knot of beast people including Slope and Lucky and BlueBob come close by. He pays little heed to them, even when BlueBob jests that each stone will be ten times as heavy by the time DogFellow has finished. When the bell actually rings he ignores that as well, and for another hour is busy, buffing the rough pumice over and over with his stout brush. Then he stops, sensing sudden movement.

First he hears the heavy bolt drawn; next the high wooden doors open and swing shut. He glances to his left and can see that it is Hector who has come out. Where is he going? It must be some business of the Master's. DogFellow doesn't know this for sure, yet in the way Hector begins to half run and half trot there is an air of unmistakable urgency. He drops the brush and straightens up. His back is hurting, revenge for the morning's toil. He pays no attention. It is Hector who absorbs him. He watches – watches through the heat haze – until the figure disappears behind the trees. What can this mean? He has no business in trying to find out. His world is now no bigger than the circumference of the bucket beside him. Yet not wanting to waste any more time, he gets to his feet and begins to follow.

It is easy enough to find the pattern that Hector's quick feet have left in the sand, although the beach ahead is deserted. The tracks run on for thirty yards or so, then curve in away from the sea, into the woods. He stops, puzzled and a little alarmed. He also feels deep inside himself the gnawing of envy, worse than a dose of the worms. The trees form a boundless phalanx, stretching away to the right as far as the eye can travel. It is the time of day when nothing stirs. Even the birds seem consumed with somnolence. Where has Hector gone? For a moment DogFellow thinks of direct pursuit, using his nose to trace that lovely, hateful mix of carbolic acid and raw alcohol. Then he thinks better: Hector will surely use the same path, in and out. So DogFellow hides, going behind a solitary palm, exiled from its massed brethren. The thin trunk affords just enough cover. He does not have long to wait. At the point where he has been standing, Hector reappears. He has something under his arm. Did he carry it before? As he goes past the tree, DogFellow steps out.

'Aghh!'

Hector is so alarmed he drops what he is bearing. Quickly DogFellow goes down to pick it up.

'Ah, DogFellow, where you come from?'

'Just there.'

He indicates some indefinite point over his shoulder. He finds he has hold of an oilskin packet, loosely folded into a square. Inside there is the rustle of paper.

'You been sleeping in the shade?' asks Hector, looking nervously about.

'Yes.'

'I haven't seen you for long time. You been hiding away?'

'No,' says DogFellow.

He slides his thumb into the folds and raises the cloth just enough to see a patch of closely scrawled foolscap.

'Sun hot today,' says Hector, conscious at last that DogFellow has no immediate intention of surrendering what was lost. When he raises his own hand a fraction, there is a corresponding turning aside on DogFellow's part. Hector opens his mouth, as if to speak. DogFellow says, 'What is this?'

'Master's business.'

'Are you taking it to him?'

'Yes . . .'

'Where did you get it?'

Hector hesitates. Then he says, 'From the Master who is not a Master.'

DogFellow, having only heard rumours of renewed dealings with the American, is desperate to know the substance of it. The desire is too great, too intemperate. He shakes off the greasy wrapper and takes hold of the contents. There are some dozen pages, each covered on both sides in black ink. He greedily eyes it. The writing is small, cramped, squeezed on to the paper. DogFellow tries to make sense of what's in front of him, labouring over the signs in the full heat of a tropical noon. He has to work hard, harder than he has all morning, though now it is with his head and his tongue. He sees words, fragments of words that he recognizes: 'go', 'he', 'I', 'strive', 'genius', but it is all too dizzying, this ghosted credo, mingling biography with an exposition on what the Master has done, will do.

'DogFellow,' whines Hector.

'I need to look for something.'

And flicking over three or four pages he attempts another block of scribble. He finds a list of words, cast in between two paragraphs that sketch out the Master's student days. He does not realize that these are names, referring to men who are twenty thousand miles away and twenty years off – dead perhaps, or broken, or else slipping into a drowsy retirement, ignorant of the peer, the student, who keeps his hatred alive and has ordered his amanuensis to make sure that a chapter is given over to detailing their every slight.

'Please, DogFellow.'

'Sshhh.'

Hector, cowed at first by the mystery of the act he is witnessing and conditioned by a certain respect for his elder, now leans in towards DogFellow. DogFellow twists around, shielding himself from interruption. He turns over the paper, fetching up another trawl of syllables. He is so intent that he gives the impression he comprehends everything, yet some words he cannot recognize at all, others he can only partly construe, patching them together as best as he is able. His eye strikes against a phrase he can snatch up, telling of human nature – human nature, that the Master has spoken of. And what does this say?

The human itself must be altered, if -

He halts, holding on to the tail of what he's found and catching his breath before plunging on:

if progress in our moral life is to match progress in the sphere of tech . . .

It is too much; his grip loosens and fails, and then the sense is gone, evaporating off the page. The words fume upwards, as dense and mobile as flies around filth. Feeling nauseated, he stops. With a sudden, awkward motion, Hector grabs the papers, pulling them out of DogFellow's hand.

'You must not see!'

A spark of aggression flies up between them and each nape bristles but there is not tinder enough in their dispositions to catch so suddenly on fire. DogFellow is the first to glance away, but only for a moment.

'So: the Master who is not a Master . . . you have been to talk with him?' he asks.

Hugging the oilskin to his chest, Hector looks like he won't answer, then he says, 'No, never talk. He leaves this, back there, by the big stone, and I find it.'

'Every day?'

'Every day the Master sends me, but every day I do not find. Sometimes the Master is angry and I take it back, so the Master who is not a Master must write it again.'

'Write it again . . .'

DogFellow is conscious of Hector's shirt, hitched up around the middle with a piece of freshly trimmed rope, but still falling down about his knees. The rolled sleeves are thread-worn, and an ancient chemical splash lies like an exclamation mark to the left of the third button down. He recognizes it, he is sure.

'I got to go now, DogFellow.'

'No. Wait –'

'What?'

He cannot bear to see Hector thus, but to let him return to the house fills him with a pang of dismay.

'You are busy with your chores?'

'Yes, yes, busy.'

'And you keep things good and clean?'

'Yes, all the time, very good, very clean.'

'Because – because you must make sure you always do things right and proper –'

Hector is already going away. DogFellow plucks at him: touches the shirt. The cotton is soft; he knows it for sure as one he has washed often, and now it has found its way on to Hector's back.

'Otherwise – otherwise –'

'I got to go.'

'Wait.'

'I got to –'

'Please.'

He says it so pathetically that Hector stops.

'I need to know. You must tell me. I –'

DogFellow hesitates, as if pained.

'What?'

'Does he ever – ever ask . . .'

He opens and shuts his mouth, turning his jaw and his tongue, but the words will not – dare not – come, because the answer has already been given, as irrevocable as black marks on paper.

'Does he . . .'

The love he continues to bear is in spasm, battering at the walls of his chest, and still the words fail him.

'Does he . . .'

Hector, who has taken his place in all that matters, glances up the beach towards his home. He stares back at DogFellow.

'Who?'

DogFellow heaves a terrible sigh. There is a moment or two more of pain, then it fades, love's struggles in abeyance.

'Who?' says Hector.

'*Him.*'

To illustrate he points towards the trees, where the fearful American purportedly lurks.

'Does he ever ask you questions? Are you sure you do not speak with the Master who is not a Master?'

'No. I told you. Sometimes I see him. But I must not, on no – *no account* – let him see me.'

He speaks from memory, repeating what has plainly been dinned into his skull.

'No, you mustn't,' says DogFellow. He releases Hector's arm, though he now has him in the fervour of his gaze. 'Beware of him. Beware of his words. He is full of lies and poison.'

'The Master has told me –'

'No!' DogFellow shouts it so loudly that he makes himself jump. Hector flinches. 'The Master does not know. Even the Master does not know what talk passes Henderson's lips.'

He speaks the man's true name as best he can, and not the tiresome formulation traded by the beast folk. He is appalled and thrilled by his own boldness, by the ring of his own words. A sudden, powerful updraught of lofty compassion – for the Master, for Hector, for all the benighted and vulnerable ignoramuses of the island – washes away his anger and jealousy.

'Beware, Hector. If he should come near you, put your fingers in your ears, because his talk is full of bad pictures: of places that are not. He tells only lies . . .'

Hector listens solemnly, then says, 'He never comes near. He does not see me. I am not afraid.'

'But he will try. And you must not let him get close. Never!'

He quivers with barely contained feeling.

'I will not,' says Hector.

'Promise me.'

Hector nods. 'I promise.'

DogFellow heaves a sigh, as if delivered of some burden.

'Good. You're a good boy, Hector.'

And with that they part and go their different ways.

Twenty

But from then on Hector cannot move without being watched. DogFellow is discreet, naturally: when he follows it is always at a distance of several yards, and in his motions he is artful, nosing out puddles of noon-tide shadow, and finding out the best places to hide, knowing that Hector – blithe and witless – will stumble past, on his way to the trysting ground. It takes DogFellow very little time to work out the pattern of transactions.

The words he saw, in their oilskin wrapper, are engaged in a sort of perpetual shuttle, between the hand of the Master and the hand of the man who is nothing, who is no one, and yet who comes to DogFellow at night, in dreams, whispering great falsehoods. Whether it is always and again the selfsame pages that are exchanged Dog-Fellow does not know, he does not think to speculate, but he sees how Hector carries paper from the house to the forest, from the forest to the house, and often-times food and ink are left, in the little hollow, by the big stone, across from the old banyan stump.

So it is: DogFellow will abandon his shrimp net or his wooden trowel at the appointed hour, and walk as if back to his hut, only to then double about, and go and wait. Several times his vigil is fruitless; once Hector, seeing a bush quiver, halts and looks, and DogFellow is obliged to retreat; but nothing comes of this and Hector carries on, unsuspecting. Yes, unsuspecting – that is it. Unlike Dog-Fellow, he does not know; he cannot see. He is as hopeless as a fish, that at high tide swims at the sea's utmost edge, oblivious to the wooden traps that have been strewn everywhere. And the Master too – is he not equally struck with this blight of not-knowing? He is God of course, he is Creator, omniscient, omnipotent, the A and the Z of island life, but still, in this – in the matter of that other man – he is as blind as a bat.

Pressing his body against the corrugated bark of the tree, DogFellow notices at once that, for the fifth day in succession, there is no packet of scribble lying in the shade of the stone. All this week he has been bold, not waiting on the path, but coming here within sight of the place, so he couldn't be mistaken or have missed anything. Soon – in a quarter of an hour or so – Hector will appear and then depart, empty-handed. DogFellow feels like leaving himself. He has deserted his fellow labourers, who still toil at the back end of morning, manuring the earth of the field with fish heads. But he cannot go, because he must stand watch, and by the very act of watching guard those others lost in their ignorance. This is what he tells himself as he hides and waits.

A sudden flash of colour catches his eye, moving in the

wall of undergrowth on the other side of the clearing. As he watches, a small parrot – small enough to perch comfortably on DogFellow's shoulder – flutters its blue and red wings and comes to rest a yard away. Its tiny black eyes swivel about, watching earth, trees and sky, and Dog-Fellow begins to wonder what it must be like to have the freedom to sweep through the air, to fly up above the island and regard it as he might a pebble by his foot, before perhaps banking on a sea breeze and passing on to who knows where. A moment later and the parrot takes fright, swooping off like a jewel cast away by some invisible hand.

'*Don't move.*'

It is Henderson, behind him.

Henderson: at last.

DogFellow is paralysed with terror and grows more terrified still when he feels a rough grasp at the back of his neck, forcing his cheek against the trunk.

'I have a knife,' says Henderson. 'I could kill you if I wanted. Are you going to struggle?'

DogFellow wants to shake his head, but can't.

'I might have known he'd try to cheat me. How like him. One out in the open, the other skulking in the bushes. I told you not to move –'

His voice is low and hoarse and puts DogFellow in mind of rusted tin.

'Who else have you got here?'

DogFellow manages to say 'No one'.

'Is he here? Is he?'

The pressure is off DogFellow's neck as Henderson steps back.

'Doctor!' he shouts. 'Doctor! Are you spying on me as well?'

'I'm alone,' says DogFellow, still staring out into the empty clearing.

'Turn about,' says Henderson. 'Turn right about.'

DogFellow does as he is told. Henderson: DogFellow has not seen him for two months and if it were not for the voice would never credit that this apparition was the same man.

'What's the matter? Did you think I was dead?'

His hair lies in thin tatters about his pink, sun-scabbed head. He has a full beard, red and grey mixed together. One of the lenses of his spectacles has a crack running across it, cutting his eye in two. His lips are flaky, with scales of whitish skin. It is not a knife he holds, but one of the machetes, its sharpened blade notched in two or three places.

'It will take more than you or your Master to see me off. I'm a little less gullible these days, as I think you'll find to your cost. Is this what you're after?'

In his other hand he has the oilskin packet containing his papers. 'Rewritten again, under the guidance of the Almighty. Do you know how many times he's made me do it? Each time I give him what he wants and each time it comes back to me covered in green pencil marks. What price perfection? He's doing it on purpose, of course. Spite, nothing but spite. Well now – it seems your little friend is late. At first I thought it was you. Brothers, are we? Bred from the same bitch?'

DogFellow, sick with fear, cannot reply.

'Planning to make a fool out of me another time – is that your game?' He leers aggressively. 'I ought to quit talking and kill you. Kill you and send him your ugly head to teach him for setting his spies on me. Are you ready for that – ready to die, you damned freak? God knows it would be just provocation. What? You have something to tell me?'

DogFellow can only manage a miserable whine.

'All right, all right,' says Henderson, and for an instance it seems as if – Yes, he is going to do it, and strike DogFellow down. But then, with a growl, he turns and stalks off a few feet. He comes back. The machete dangles loosely in his hand.

'I tell you what's going to happen here. You are going to help me, yes, you are , whether you want to or not.'

There is a sudden rustling in the undergrowth. Henderson sets the flat of the machete blade across DogFellow's mouth and watches as a moment later Hector appears in the clearing and goes to the place where the papers should be. He peers about and even reaches down into the shallow depression, as if the oilskin wrapper had turned invisible and might only be discovered by touch. Realizing that today will again be barren, he leaves a little food, though only a little, which reflects the Master's irritation with the tardiness of the author. Then Hector goes back the way he came. The only sound remaining is the see-sawing of breath between DogFellow and Henderson.

Henderson again drops his weapon, his uncracked eye roving back and forth.

'What is going on? Who were you really watching for: him or me?'

'Him.'

He almost chokes on the word.

'Why would you do that?'

DogFellow gnaws at the thin rind of his lower lip.

'Come on, quick: answer me. What's it about? I swear if you don't tell me why you're here . . .'

He lifts his blade waist-high. DogFellow tries to retreat and bumps the back of his head against the tree.

'Well?' demands Henderson.

'Because he does not understand.'

'Understand what?'

'The – the things – you say.'

Henderson screws up his eyes, as if he could see into DogFellow's head and rifle through his thoughts.

'What does that mean, the things I say?'

'The other places – not here – not here – but far away . . .'

'Is that so?'

'Yes. Yes.'

'You understand, though, don't you?'

DogFellow nods.

'You cleverer than he is?'

'Yes.'

'So why is he running the errands these days and not you?'

'I . . . I was sick,' says DogFellow. 'The Master, he did not need me . . .'

'Oh, I get it. You got the push. Tough luck. So we're both in the same boat now, eh?'

'Same boat?' murmurs DogFellow, vaguely stirred.

'Cast out of the paradise of his divine presence. Ha! It's a blessing, believe me. If I had half a chance . . . well, I wouldn't keep on writing this garbage. But I've been made to compromise. Quid pro quo: I supply the words and he provides the dietary extras. Man cannot live by fish alone. I got a tin of peaches last week. Go on – go make yourself useful. Fetch me what your friend left.'

DogFellow turns about and with a slow, deliberate tread, which disguises the tremor in his legs, walks to the stone. He brings back half a coconut. In the white concavity there is a twist of newspaper. At the sight of the coconut Henderson gives a scowl of distaste.

'See, this is what I mean. This is the bastard he is. Where's the consistency? I wanted tobacco, or chocolate even. He *knows* that. Goddamn coconut! Does he think it's some kind of joke? Are you laughing at me, doctor?'

He snatches it up in a sudden fury and throws it into the bushes, as if he could see his tormentor standing there, enjoying the scene. But he keeps the paper and, undoing it, mutters something. He tips the contents – no more than a heaped teaspoon of sugar – into his mouth. He closes his eyes and for a moment his expression relaxes.

'Oh it's good, it's good,' he murmurs, before recalling himself. He snorts in disgust. 'Can you believe what he's reduced me to? He probably swept it up off the kitchen floor as well. What a swine! I ought to show him –'

He stares at the precious package he carries, seeming to weigh it in his hands while a range of conflicted thoughts and feelings play out across his raddled, wretched-looking face. But if he has any impulse to rip it up, this passes. Instead, he turns to studying DogFellow.

'Take it. Go on. Into the hole with it.'

When this act has been performed, Henderson nods approvingly. His entire mood is different.

'A little cooperation: isn't that all I ever asked for?'

'Cooperation,' repeats DogFellow, still frightened. Nodding, Henderson passes the square of newsprint to him. Adhering to the murky surface, scattered between the words, are a few small square grains.

'Here,' says the Master who is not a Master, 'you have it.'

Understanding that somehow he must, DogFellow pokes out the tip of his tongue and, like a hummingbird at the flower, delicately dabs off the tiny morsels.

'Tastes good, don't it? That's also called cooperation. What's sweet for me can be sweet for you. Men understand that. Proper men. Free men.'

DogFellow licks his lips, where the delicious flavour remains.

'Nice, hey?'

'Nice.'

'You follow my line of thinking, don't you?'

'I-I follow,' says DogFellow, able to echo this new, peculiar idiom, although grasping little of its portent. The very fact that the anger is out of Henderson's manner is incentive enough.

'So we can trust each other?'

'Trust each other.'

'Yes, you see things straight enough. I was on the right track from the second I set eyes on you. You're no numbskull. No; you're like me. We're the same: the same. He's betrayed us both. But every dog will have its day – right?'

He gives a sudden alarming grin, showing off his dirty teeth; then quite suddenly he turns and starts to walk away, letting leaves and branches swish shut behind him. DogFellow waits in a silent fury of indecision, as ripe to do one thing as another – more likely indeed to let the green curtain settle, shutting off Henderson from view. But then, through the vegetative tangle, he can make out the way the man pauses and casts his eyes back, looking at DogFellow, looking *into* him, and as quick as that he runs along, the way that Henderson has gone.

Twenty-one

They take a circuitous route, though it is evident from
Henderson's stride that he knows the contours of the land.
The path leads up over a ridge and then into a narrow
defile, cut as if by a giant blade. Henderson limps slightly
and he swings his machete as he goes, chipping branches
and sending leaves tumbling in his wake. It is not difficult
to follow him; the blind could do it, he makes so much
noise. DogFellow is careful to keep him just in sight and
constantly glances from side to side and once or twice
behind himself. After a time he wonders if Henderson is
at all aware he is being followed, and this thought alarms
him: should he call after him? Then the ground begins
to slope. The smell of the sea grows more pungent and
soon can be seen, sifted through the final outcrop of forest.
Henderson has already cleared the last few yards and
stands on the shore, looking still more unkempt with the
raw afternoon light battering down on him. The expression he has on his face is indecipherable to DogFellow, but
from the way he signals with his blade it is plain there is

no surprise in discovering this queer loping figure, half in the woods, half in the open.

'Quickly. Over here.'

DogFellow dares to tread on the crumbling sand, hot to his bare feet. Shielded on either side by overgrown lobes of volcanic stone the scrap of sand seems utterly forlorn, a thousand miles from anything familiar.

'To me.'

Henderson has wandered down to a natural bench of rock, positioned a yard or so from the bubble and swish of the outgoing tide. He sits down and tilts his head up to the sky, blinking. DogFellow comes closer, though he is still painfully wary.

'You know,' says Henderson, as if to the air, 'I always considered it a romantic kind of notion, to be marooned on a desert island. There'd be palm trees and macaws and a waterfall where you could scrub yourself clean. Nothing to do all day but laze in the sun, eating pineapples – paw-paws – maybe some fine-looking native girl, born beyond the reach of shame.'

He closes his eyes, perhaps to make the vision sharper. DogFellow is near enough to see the texture of his sandy eyelashes beneath the fractured glasses.

'I was brought up on a farm, in the middle of nowhere. All I dreamed about was escaping. Sometimes life just seems to go in circles, don't you find? Round and round, taking you with it, unless you can find a way of jumping clear. Coming here was supposed to be my way out. Instead of which . . . ah, what the hell. I can still make something out of it.'

He stops talking and scratches his beard and it's as if he's aware again of the mute spectator, who listens so quietly and patiently to all this relentless thinking out loud. Henderson suddenly says, 'Do you want to see something?' and before DogFellow is aware that a yes or no ought to be vouchsafed the man has rolled up his filthy, threadbare trouser leg.

'Look at that,' he says. The ulcer is a shallow depression in the thin shank of his calf. It glistens yellow and red.

'I tell you,' he says, covering it up again, 'if I have to stay on this island much longer I'm going to die. Is that what you want?'

DogFellow wrinkles his nose, smelling the odour of septic tissue carried to him on the breeze.

'I should have been home two, three months ago, instead of which I find myself working like some scribe for old Pharaoh, writing out page after page of bilge and nonsense. Memoirs of the man-god. Hah! Half of it you can't begin to understand, and the other half you wouldn't want to. You know that you're just the first step – that he wants to set about changing people next? Move 'em up a grade, as he sees it. Calls himself magus. Wants the world to listen. Well, when I get off this island the world will listen all right, but not in the way he's thinking. Greatest story of my career, just you wait and see. Bigger than I could have hoped. Whichever way it falls I'm coming out of this ahead of the pack. They'll know my name. It's stupendous really. Hey, you, pay attention.'

Henderson suddenly points straight ahead, to where the further lobe of land drops into the sea.

'Due east, a little north maybe. Four or five weeks by steamship, perhaps less, and that's it. That's home! Hot baths, hotels, steak dinners and clean linen. Everything that money can buy and the money to buy it with –'

He stares at the far horizon. DogFellow watches Henderson's back, seeing the bony plane of a shoulder blade through a rip in his shirt. After a little while he ventures to ask 'It is . . . it is the same, like in Paris?'

'No. It's better,' says Henderson, as if to the sea.

'And . . . and the ladies . . . they are very be-autiful?'

DogFellow speaks awkwardly, venturing words he has only ever uttered to himself.

'Very,' says Henderson, still addressing the Pacific.

'And do they have hats, in the gardens?'

Henderson's shoulders twitch. He leaves his bench and walks a little way along the shore.

'What gardens?'

'The Paris gardens.'

'Is that what he's taught you?'

'No.'

DogFellow sounds emphatic, as if he resents such an imputation.

'Well, if you want to know, the ladies all have hats, very fine hats. Even the poor ugly ones have their hats. And if they wear them anywhere – well, why not in the garden, Paris or otherwise. But what's all that to you?'

The question – indeed, everything in the American's constantly shifting demeanour – is confusing to DogFellow.

'In Paris –' he repeats.

'In Paris, in Paris,' parrots Henderson. 'You talk about

it, but when are you going to act on it? I'm dying here, dying day by day and so are you – at least the part of you that's worth saving. You tell me you want to go to Paris?'

DogFellow stays silent, overpowered by what has been so casually queried.

To go to Paris –

He is where he is, by the rock, but at the same time he is in that other place, in all its black and white splendour.

'Look. Listen.'

Henderson now comes so near that his odour blots out the endless nuances of sea smell.

'Either we go or we stay. I can't do it on my own. If I could I would, but I don't have a gun – *he* does. I've seen him out the back, looking through his spyglass, watching and waiting. Oh, he's made me promises – new ones. If I fulfil my original obligation, blah blah blah, he'll fix me up with my return passage . . . He must think I'm greener than the grass. Sure, I'll play along for now, but I'm certainly not fool enough to fall into any more of his traps. He never wants me to leave. Which is why I need you to help me. We can go together, see? You and me, all the way back home.'

DogFellow gives a faint nod.

'The two of us. You don't belong here any more than I do.'

Henderson touches the top of DogFellow's head. Dog-Fellow does not recoil. Instead he lets the hand rub back and forth over the wiry stubble that cakes his scalp: back and forth, back and forth. There is great comfort to be had in this, and at the same time the man's voice comes to him like the lapping of the waves. If he shuts his eyelids the light grows soft too, and as pink as the inside of a seashell.

Oh Master –

The hand is gone, and there is Henderson, standing in front of him.

'So this is how it's going to be,' he is saying. 'You find out the time of the next ship, whether it's Captain van Toch or not. It was the *Kandong Bandoeng* that brought me. Listen out; it might be back again any day. See if you catch him mentioning it. You let me know as soon – as soon – as you have the slightest clue. Light a fire – no, don't do that – get a note to me – you can write, can't you? Just a line will do it –'

It goes on in this vein for some while. Is it really happening? The bite of a fly on the top side of his left hand convinces DogFellow that this is more than mere imagination. He agrees with everything Henderson demands of him.

'Good,' says Henderson at last. 'We'll spring ourselves from this rat-trap. Only remember what you promised. Not a word, not to him, or to any of the others. They'll get their chance later. He'll get his too, the crazy bastard. Everything's going to be settled one way or another.'

Transported by his own giddy thoughts he takes a turn about the beach, stopping to pick up a lump of stone.

'Just you wait.'

DogFellow watches as Henderson hurls the stone out to sea. It falls with a plop.

'Freedom, freedom, freedom!' shouts the man. 'Freedom and dinners!'

And his voice floats high, and far away –

Twenty-two

'Hey, DogFellow,' says Hector.

For a week now, DogFellow has followed him only with his eyes, glancing up from whatever job that needs doing. This day he is wearily chopping at an ancient tree stump, uncovered in the corner of the breadfruit field. The roots lie matted about the dead core and the art is to tease out the earth, so that the mass is exposed to lie in the air like a fossilized octopus. It goes slowly, however, and DogFellow makes it slower still, seeking to absorb himself in the rivulets of earth that spill down between the root mass as he undermines it. But now Hector comes up, with his stupid grin, standing at the edge of the hole DogFellow has made.

'You digging up the garden?' he asks.

Looking up and shading his brow with his forearm, DogFellow says, 'You see what I do.'

'Pretty good job too, DogFellow.'

'Another hour and I will pull it up.'

'Hey! You been getting pretty strong since you been out

of doors. Me, I get weaker all the time. Too much indoors – that's Hector's problem.'

DogFellow, who never complained once during all his time in the Master's service, snorts derisively. Then he says, 'What you doing here anyway?'

'Oh, Master does not need me today.'

The words are like a physical blow in DogFellow's belly.

'Why not?' he asks, almost not daring to stay and hear the answer.

'Don't know,' says Hector cheerily. 'He just told me to go away this afternoon and not come back till, um, day after tomorrow.'

'The ship,' croaks DogFellow. '*Kandong Bandoeng*. *Kangdong Bandoeng*: the ship that brings the animals. Is – is it coming?'

Hector raises his shoulders in some approximation of a shrug. He fails to notice the signs of DogFellow's agitation.

'Master never say nothing, old chap. No *Kingdong Bingbong* or what you call it. I just leave, quick as you like, in time for dinner. You come to eat now?'

DogFellow, staring at the wood scraper in his dirty hands, mutters something inaudible.

'We got to hurry up or other greedy beasts will take all the best things. If you like, later, I help you pull the root, but now we need to go and fetch our plates. Hey, Dog-Fellow: you listening to Hector?'

Summoned back, DogFellow can see nothing for it but to pump Hector for any clue. So, stiff and awkward, he half climbs and is half pulled out of the trench he has made. As they walk eastwards towards the House of Food they continue to talk, DogFellow enquiring as best he can about the Master (has he been busy of late about the cages, for example) while Hector continues to be infuriatingly vacant, revealing a lack of perspicacity that DogFellow can scarcely credit. He only laughs merrily at his own ignorance, turning it all into a joke, and in this style – the one all smiles, the other fretful – they join the line. Once they have received their dole DogFellow would slip away, to eat by himself and think on Henderson and what might be done, but Hector says, 'No, no, you cannot go be by yourself this day. We sit together, like proper good friends. Ho, you lazy beast there,' he exclaims at the occupant of the shadiest spot, 'you shift up along for DogFellow and me.'

The other – a thing of unguessable provenance – scowls over its shoulder, but recognizes who it is that asks and budges accordingly.

'Now,' says Hector, 'we can eat our scoff,' and, side by side, they hunker down and spoon up the stew. Dog-Fellow has little appetite, however, and after a few mouthfuls merely stirs at the residue, nodding only when Hector's empty banter requires some endorsement. Every attempt to find out if the Master is readying himself to receive a new shipment leads nowhere. He is about to summon up an excuse to go when suddenly Fantine appears and squats directly opposite.

'Hello, DogFellow,' she says.

He takes another tepid spoonful of his dinner and mumbles his reply.

'What you doing here with him?'

'Can't friends be friendly?' interrupts Hector.

'DogFellow has no friends.'

'I am DogFellow's friend.'

'So you may think –'

'I do think. He and me, we are brothers. Any beast who don't say yes is a dirty rascal. Isn't that true, old chap?'

He turns to DogFellow for support, but DogFellow is occupied in stirring his meal.

Fantine smiles at this and licks the back of her spoon, though it has not yet been wetted in the bowl.

'Don't be angry with me, Hector,' she says. 'I am glad to see such a sight. You go well together, like two monkeys sitting up a tree. It is hard to tell one from another.'

'Hey –' begins Hector, aware that this must constitute an insult of sorts. DogFellow begins to stand.

'Oh forgive me,' says Fantine. 'I have got it wrong. I am such a fool. It is *we* who are the monkeys, not Dog-Fellow.'

'What monkeys?' asks Hector, now confused.

'It is nothing,' says DogFellow.

'You have not heard?' asks Fantine in mock surprise. 'DogFellow is not as we are. He is better by far. Can't you see it? Look at his hands: see? See how fine they are? They smell like flowers –'

Before Hector can find out if this is true or not Dog-Fellow has got to his feet. Without a word he walks off, pushing past a draggle of latecomers.

'Oh, DogFellow,' calls Fantine, 'Oh do not forget your hat and your cane!'

The peal of her mocking laughter seems to follow him for ages afterwards.

DogFellow waits one day, two days, wondering if the ship will come, and in that time he is unable to think or act. Should he go and find the place where he and Henderson talked – where they made their pact? Yes, he tells himself, yes – and yet he does nothing. On the third day Hector returns to the compound, and still DogFellow continues to lie in an agony of uncertainty. The tree root remains lodged in the earth. He merely prods at it, knocks at it, studies its dull serpentine course. It seems to mock him with its heaviness, just as Fantine mocked, except in her airs and demeanour she is entirely the opposite – quick, sharp and stinging.

At last, unable to bear it any longer, he throws down his digger and walks north to where the ground rises. It is a restless impulse. He goes halfway, then stops and begins to turn back. The noon light is brilliant and falls through the tree cover, leopard-spotting the ground at his feet and making the leaves glow. Sniffing the air, he finds something strange. He follows the odour, continuing to retrace his steps. He can smell burning. It tickles his nostrils, pricking the ultra-fine inner membranes. Like a spider in its web, he moves towards the point of disturbance. Above the compound, close to the main gate, a curious heat haze shimmers. A moment later and the air's gelatinous quivering grows much darker and then, all at once, there is a flash of orange, bright even against the brightness of the day.

Only at this does DogFellow react, giving a startled yip and jumping into a awkward run, first one way and then the other, until sense sends him skittering across the assembly field as fast as his legs can carry him. He tries to shout and nothing comes out – just a reverse gulp, void of content. Once more, and the ragged edges of a word flap uselessly on the warm, still air. By now he is running parallel to the wall and it is so quiet it might be a dream. He turns the corner, to where the compound fronts the sea, and is terrified that the gate will be locked. He runs at the nearest door and is carried forward, full tilt, as it swings inward.

The heat is instantly upon him, like a wave, and his ears are full of the rumble of fire. The wash hut – blessed to memory – is no more, surviving only as a blur in the midst of an upwards rushing torrent of destruction. He has to draw back as he feels his own skin begin to dry and crackle in time with the crackling of incinerated timbers. When he looks up to where the torrent leads he sees a widening pall of black smoke and – far worse – a flurry of molten cinders, rising upwards and outwards. Still it seems a dream, as he ransacks his mind to explain how his world has come to flaming ruin, and only then does it occur to him that it is Hector who now tends to the wash pot – that it is his domain.

'Hector!'

DogFellow makes an ineffectual dash forward, and while no voice makes answer the fire itself signals by pulling the roof inward with a mighty whoosh and ten thousand sparks burst into frantic life. Some land on him and he has to slap them dead while hopping backwards to escape the soaring temperature. Another inward eructation sends the entire structure of the building lurching rightwards and already a nearby water-butt is beginning to steam and smoulder.

He runs towards the rear of the house and with a bang, bang, he assaults the door, feeling it shudder and rattle. The latch gives a sterile clack, the inside bolt holding fast. DogFellow kicks with his bare foot, gives a flurry of kicks, and while he kicks he shouts, and the heat at his back makes him wild with fear. The door yields. He thinks it is his own strength, but then the Master is standing there, the scar of a pillow seam angled across one flushed cheek. He seems huge, appalling, half naked. DogFellow, even in the throes of being roasted, staggers back in awe and terror. The Master's arms are whiter than even his finest cotton shirts; his barrel chest is smooth, like a stone in water. For a few moments he looks lost, hauled up from the deep well of an afternoon's forty winks, and then the putty of his face moulds itself into an expression of outright alarm. He pushes past DogFellow as if intending to immolate himself, unhitched braces and all, in the raging pyre. He runs close on his big bare feet, shielding his face with an upraised hand. He quickly sizes up the situation and, hopping to and fro on his burned soles, goes to the main gates and sets them wide. Then he turns and is shouting, and it seems he would put out the flames by the force of his Olympian rage, until DogFellow realizes that it is he who is being shouted at.

The fear of fire is elemental, but the fear of the Master lies encoded, grained in his flesh like the grain in wood. Together they sweat and struggle to pull clear the stack of loose crates crammed with packing straw that lie perilously close to the burning hulk of the wash house. Then the Master runs back indoors and returns wearing a shirt and boots. He speaks; gives commands.

'Damn you, hop to it! Get the others. Tell them all to come and help. Quick as you can! Now!'

Returning to the queer condition of his afternoon dream, DogFellow goes out through the gates on cotton-wool legs and takes the path to the dinner hut. As he scuttles along he shouts out, 'Fire! Fire!', although the fountain of smoke and flame rising up behind him tells this story clearly enough. A few beast people come towards him, already startled by the stink of burning. He gasps out some barely coherent instructions, urging attendance on the embattled Master, and then continues his journey, swinging westwards this time. Another knot of six or seven meet him on the way to the fields.

'Go – quick – fire – Master – danger – help –'

He scatters words like beads from a broken necklace and, without waiting to see if anything is understood, carries on along the track, through the brown and green geometry of cultivation and out the other side. The compound is now lost to view, the chaotic sounds of destruction existing merely as an after-echo. There is no one else to be seen. DogFellow slows and halts, riding the violent up-and-down rattle of his chest. If he looks back he can make out only a tall column of darkness. He walks on another ten yards, seeing in his head the Master's bare white body and the shivering mass of flame. He thinks perhaps it is indeed a dream he has had before, and is having again now. Perhaps it is all a dream and he will wake up somewhere else as something else.

Pricked by thirst, he sniffs out a ditch and, on his knees, plunges his head into the reedy trough, lapping at the stagnant water. He surfaces, choking on filth. He spits it out and claws a hank of weed from the side of his face. When he lifts his gaze, he sees how the river of smoke seems to have got denser and pours up into the sky with relentless vigour. He starts to run towards it, as fast as he can.

The beast people have formed a chain, which – as if designed for this very purpose – can just stretch from the topmost line of the surf to the wide open portals of the compound. Up and down the line pass a range of household and medical receptacles, swept up into service by the Master, who stands and bawls at his creation. A bowl heavy with sea water jumps from one hand to another, ending its passage in the grip of BearCreature, who just about remembers to throw the contents only into the orange belly of the fire. The task complete, he turns and goes back to the end of the chain, recharging his vessel in the surf. DogFellow, his eyes damp with relief to find that living order has prevailed over death and smoking ruin, would slip unseen among the others and play his part but the Master is ever vigilant and whistles him over.

'Go to the front and make sure they throw straight – got it?'

DogFellow licks his lips with the taste of stagnancy still on them and does as he is told. As the fire dwindles it leaves a sodden blackness behind. At last it goes out altogether. The Master says nothing as he stands before the smouldering wreckage. He turns to look at DogFellow, then past DogFellow, and his eyes narrow, his brows lower. DogFellow dares to look himself and is amazed – astonished – relieved – to see Hector standing on the outskirts of the crowd of beasts. Whereas many of them carry some mark of close engagement with the conflagration – a sooty stain, a scorch mark even, worn on the face or the arms – Hector is untouched, yet the expression he wears is anything but blithe. DogFellow's glance wanders across to Fantine, who has also, it seems, appeared from nowhere. Does DogFellow already suspect? Is this where the future is made? Yet at this moment all is blotted out by the dreadful expectation of violence: the horror, which is almost a pleasure, of being an innocent witness.

'You.'

The Master mouths it and Hector quails, seeing all too plainly the consequences of his neglect.

'Come here.'

A breathless murmur follows him as, on unstrung knees, he creeps forward. Whatever is dog in him now rises up, betraying itself in his toothy grimace, in the submissive twist of his low-slung head.

'Closer.'

Back arched, the thick hair on his head and the thin hair on his nape folded smooth, Hector enters the ambit of sudden, lightning-fast retribution. Yet for now the Master stands, arms folded.

'Why did you leave the fire untended?' he asks.

Between clenched teeth, Hector manages to say, 'The fire burn and burn down to a little. I thought he nearly gone away . . .'

DogFellow winces inwardly: best not to offer any shred of defence; best to fall grovelling to the floor –

'I told you to never leave the fire. Never, not even smouldering. Do you see what your carelessness and neglect have achieved?'

'*Yeeess,*' says Hector, the word drawn out into a long whine.

The Master exhales through his lips, his disgust palpable.

'I ought to hang you from the next tree. Put a rope about your neck and let you swing. My shirts – my shirts . . .' He shakes his head. 'You damned confounded imbecile.'

As he takes a step closer, Hector's legs fold altogether and he topples on to his back, a picture of wretched subjugation.

'Up!'

Hector, mewling, wriggles in the dirt.

'Up, I said!'

Hector struggles into a squat.

'You will go and stand on the beach. Go and stand

right over there, where I can see you. And you think about what you've done!'

Hector, still bowed over, scuttles off. He might even want to keep moving and disappear beneath the sea, except the Master calls after him, and he has to halt right there, and later he can be seen, even as the stars are coming out. Around his neck is a piece of string, tied at either end to a strip of flimsy wood. On the strip of wood something has been written. It says IDIOT DOG. The other beasts cannot read it, but they smell the stink of ignominy well enough. Some watch as the Master hangs it there. At his side, keeping pace with him as he strides back up the beach, is a figure that from a distance could be mistaken for Hector's own.

Except, of course, it is not Hector.

DogFellow looked out across the sea and watched a big frigate bird plunge down to strike at something. It folded its wings in tight against its body and went in fast, like a dropped pebble. After a few moments it reappeared, gulping. The tail of a fish stuck up out of its beak and then vanished. Out of the corner of his eye he could see three beast people frolicking near the surf. One repeatedly ran in circles on his hands and knees, yacking with hilarity, while the two others hurled fistfuls of wet sand on to his bare body. DogFellow tried to ignore their existence, but by their actions and their noise they insisted on intruding.

'I hope the sun burns your backs off,' he muttered to himself, and he considered how they would not come for the Master, yet turn up eagerly enough to make idiots of themselves.

Fools, halfwits, cockroaches! He knew what they were all right. His head ached with the strain of staring at the water. His eyes burned with the effort. All of them – the egregious BlueBob, a pig-man, and some small, rat-like *creature DogFellow had hardly ever acknowledged – mixed their voices, robbed of sense, to a general din. He might go across and attempt to speak, try to snag some corner of awareness, and then either rebuke them directly, or choose a more roundabout course, such as asking where their trousers were, and what they intended to say when He came back, but such strategies had been tried before, tried uncounted times, and had stopped nothing and yielded less. Weeks had gone by; weeks that must now be counted in months (he would try, though his numbering skills were weak) and all about him they'd continued their slide.*

When they had tired of their game they would retire from the beach and go back into the forest, where they lived, every one. Such clothes as still hung upon them – a bit of shirt, a rope tied around the middle – were kept by accident, not design, in the same way that a patch of cloth caught on thorns might stay there, until the sun and the wind and the rain consumed it. Their cups and plates were lost; the spoons they once ate with had disappeared. Now they fed when they could, on what they might, showing no memory for the House of Food, or its rules. To watch them at their grub was to be disgusted. They had all the regard for nicety and scruple that the bats showed when zigzagging after insects on the back of evening, except that bats knew no better and at least cloaked their prey beneath their wings, consuming it thus. In contrast, the beast people (and he wondered how long that name could last, before uncoupling forever) would squat in full view and cram their mouths with worms and leaves and whatever else they might nose out.

DogFellow shook his head: weary, weary. And worst of all they were forgetting – had forgotten – how to make language, letting their store of words rot down to a scattering of useless syllables and decayed fragments, which might never again be swept up and formed into something whole.

'Uh–mum–mum–ah-a-ah-babababa-aba-pahpahpah.'

In such a manner they babbled, one to another, trading senseless rubbish and laughing with imbecile pleasure. If they fingered their own excrement and smeared it on their cheeks DogFellow could not consider it any more base or lowly.

'Mmnnf – hahaha!'

How could any of them be considered persons any more, if they were no longer able to trade strings of words, bartering sense about the island? DogFellow guarded his own language warily, keeping careful vigil by it. It was still there, all of it, and as if to prove the fact he began a recitation of the alphabet, telling off each individual letter, feeling its contours in his mouth – rounded, spiky, sleek, buzzing – and simultaneously striving to picture it, as if it was carved out of wood or stone. He corralled them all, from A, B, and C down all the way to Z, putting every one in order, to the exact place it belonged: M between L and N, the T after S, F before G – or should it be H? He experienced a moment's anxiety, and had to start again from the very beginning, letting the heavy tread of his muttering lead him to the conclusion that it truly was F, G, H.

Still the three who were annoying DogFellow to distraction continued their game, slapping each other with lazy abandon. They showed no interest in him whatsoever, being neither afraid nor abashed. Once before he'd grown so vexed that he ran at a crowd of them, waving his arms and bawling at the top of his voice. To his relief they had fled, but not far, and afterwards they'd joined up again, and he was made uncomfortably aware of their proximity, their eyes set on him always, as if they could sense his strangeness. It was then that he perhaps might have understood what 'irrevocable' meant, as surely as if he'd looked it up in the Master's old leather-bound dictionary, a tome still in existence, although crumbling on its shelf, the spoil of tropical fungi and hungry insects. Words, it seemed, could not last for long in any shape or form on this island.

The creatures, who were closer again now, seemed still intent upon their idiocy. Creatures: that is what they were called. He decided it there and then. Not persons, but creatures. Where had the persons disappeared to? They had simply gone: gone with the clothes, gone with the spoons, gone with the language of the Law. As if – as if a great wind had blown across the sea, and torn up by the roots everything that mattered, the precious, the invisible, sweeping it away, and leaving only lumber behind. Where did it all end up? DogFellow could not say.

Still they yammered and cavorted. Perhaps he was now so much a feature of this part of the beach – close to the tumbling rocks, away from the house – that he had joined the geography of the place, and might in time be included in their games, as a point to run towards or hunker down behind.

Just let them try it, he thought.

He returned to his ocean vigil. The frigate bird floated on the water, its long hooked beak resting on its red bosom. There were no others of its kind anywhere near. As he looked, DogFellow remembered a particular knife he'd once glimpsed, that was so sharp and so special that it had its own wooden box, where it slept on a crimson cushion. It was as if that knife were inside him now, working away – but that could not be, for the pain he felt was as dull as the bass boom of the faraway surf.

What, then, must it all mean?

The creature formerly known as BlueBob threw back his head and went 'Ya-ya-dwit-me-hee-hee-hee!'

Twenty-three

'Come here a minute,' says the Master for the second time. It is morning again, and DogFellow is sweeping a band of suds across the damp floorboards of the laboratory, thinking about ships and the man who crouches in his cave and waits.

'I said, come here.'

Some days have passed since his restoration, and the mindless joy that first possessed him has now gone away, to be replaced by different thoughts entirely. He has tried to tell himself that none of it happened – that it has been a wayward reverie – but in his heart he knows that something has passed between himself and Henderson – and that something is expected.

'What's wrong with you?'

He does not want to, but he must consider the possibility – the probability – that somehow the non-existent pact DogFellow never struck will come to the Master's notice, and before DogFellow can explain there will be a dreadful misunderstanding and the truth will count for nothing . . .

'Are you deaf?'

He swirls his stout brush in his bucket of dirty water and it's as if the sud-strewn vortex he makes is an image of the spin he is in, thrown round and around in an ever-dilating circle of dread. He submerges his hand to the elbow, and presses his knuckles against the bucket's metal bottom, trying to gain a purchase on the surface of things. A *harumph* from behind him and the stomp of feet bring him back to an absolute sense of the Master's presence.

'Will you deliberately disobey me?'

Now, looking up into that stern and terrible face, he is seized at once by the desire to tell everything, to reveal how it is that Henderson might soon be coming with twisted words and that he, DogFellow, although perhaps guilty of trusting too much and talking too freely, has never owned anything but pure, unquenchable love, dancing like a flame in his heart –

So acute is the compunction that he drops his brush and prepares to speak. Then, as quickly as it rose up in him, the feeling passes. His mind lets in the tiniest morsel of a scene – the aftermath of his fumbling, half-understood explanation – and no sooner is it admitted than the rest follows and he wilts before the power of his own imagination. The Master understands everything, yet he will not understand this. He has a thousand eyes it's true, but he will not see what matters . . .

'What on earth is wrong with you?'

'No wrong, Master,' says DogFellow.

He shakes his head. Then he says, 'Well, pull yourself together. I need you to go out for a little while.'

DogFellow does not speak and does not move. The Master is indifferent to this.

'It shouldn't take long, but I need to explain –'

His attention is briefly taken by the wayward flight of a little bug, coming in over his shoulder and cutting across his eye-line. He flaps at it, catches it, studies it for a few seconds and then decides to let it go, so it can fly back the way it came.

'Stand up; stop grovelling.'

DogFellow gets to his feet.

'What is it, Master?' he asks.

'There's something I need you to fetch for me. Something important. I need to be able to rely on you.'

'Yes, Master.'

'I need you to be as quick as you can.'

'Yes, Master.'

'Will you concentrate and do exactly as I tell you?'

'Yes, yes!'

He is ready to be off: next door, into the yard, even braving the hated infirmary. He will show by his alacrity just how good he can be. The Master reads his intent and steadies him with a second shake of the head.

'No. Wait. This is different. You are to go into the forest.'

Oh!

Has DogFellow been found out? The possibility is telegraphed across the arc of his brain-case and he feels the floor he has been scrubbing jump beneath his bare feet. But if the Master suspects anything he does not indicate the fact. Instead of levelling accusations he is simply telling DogFellow how he must proceed, journeying down towards the stand of palms that nod and sway together like idle gossips, and then turning due north – north, and nothing else – before following the trail until, by the hulk of a rotten banyan, he will find a small clearing (he cannot miss it) and in the middle of the clearing a large stone . . .

He talks as if he has no inkling of what DogFellow might know and DogFellow lends his ear as if this belief were not misplaced, consciously putting on those facial expressions which might be taken to connote ignorance and innocence combined. At this he works slightly too hard, because the Master has to interrupt himself as he is explaining about the half bottle of ink and punnet of figs to ask, 'What in the blazes *is* the matter with you?'

'Nothing, Master,' says DogFellow falsely. 'Figs, and ink –'

'Yes, figs and ink, you fool. You simply leave them and bring me whatever you find already left there. It will be a packet, wrapped in waterproof cloth. You'll find it easily enough if it's there. I hope to God it is, for his sake . . .'

Up until this point Henderson has not been mentioned at all, and now it is only as a third-person pronoun, so that the Master might still be narrating the miraculous properties of an enchanted forest, which receives titbits and writing materials and yields in return page after page of finished scribble, except that even the scribble is not specified: DogFellow has simply to find what is there and bring it back.

'Look in the hollow by the stone,' he is told. 'Be as quick as you can. And if anyone –' DogFellow swallows his breath – 'if anyone tries to talk to you, don't answer back.'

Outside it is a little hazy, and the air seems to catch in the nose and the back of the throat. A couple of beast people are loitering down by the edge of the flat sea, their rakes loosely shouldered. DogFellow cannot make out who they are, but they recognize him, coming out of the main gates with a bundle under his arm, and they immediately fall about their interrupted business, making for the fields. He is too preoccupied to notice or care.

Rather than elect to draw out the task by a leaden-footed traipse, he hurries forward, traversing from east to west as fast as he is able – not running, but going at a lick, making himself begin to pant. He knows the way all too well, of course. The Master's words are superfluous. He leaves the sand and soon finds the path that runs north like a dirt-brown snake between the trees and bushes. If he is fast, in and out, then (he tells himself) no harm can befall. The birds call overhead. A branch catches his ear, flicking forward, then back. Already he can glimpse the clearing, and he lets the bundle drop from the crook of his arm into his hands. He clears the final yard and immediately sees, done up as before, the proof that Henderson has already visited: perhaps days before, perhaps minutes. The ink and figs are set down; the packet is collected, and he's away again, back to the beach. He thinks he can feel eyes on himself and a shudder goes up his back, the way a spear in the water might move when a fish is run right the way through, yet he does not shift the tempo he has set himself, going along the dirt-brown snake in the same determined manner. Only when he's clear of the forest does he break the pace and let the shivers leave the locus of his spine and go along his arms and across the nape and base of his skull. He has done precisely what he had to do, in exact accordance with the Master's desire, and the old familiar oilskin pouch is clutched to his chest. Perhaps Henderson still watches him. Perhaps he thinks that this is Hector. Perhaps he knows DogFellow when he sees him and is content to wait. Perhaps, perhaps . . .

Suddenly, by the rustling palms, he stops dead. Something new has coalesced out of the darkness: a dangerous trick he has hitherto never considered, but which now seem nearby and full of threat. He pulls the manuscript away from its skin and stares at it, looking at the top sheet, plucking at the letters that are woven into words, that are meshed into sentences, that lie adjacent to one another like the tines of a fork.

What does it say?

Show this page – any page – to the beast people who lumber and limp about the island and there would be no greater response than might be granted to a handful of sand: only the fleeting acknowledgement of small particles running together, and possibly not even that. Yet show it to him, to DogFellow, and he will instantly begin to interpret, discovering the invisible and majestic republic of thought that is miraculously carried on the back and the belly of a single piece of paper, imbued in every upright, crossbar and curl of black. And yet today the miracle is recalcitrant. Though he scrutinizes the paper, lifting it so close to his face that the smells it gives off make his doggish senses reel, he can manage only an 'and', an 'island', a 'return', before losing his thread: the labyrinth closes in upon him and he's lost amidst shapes he cannot begin to elucidate. What do these signs tell him? He is in no fit state to sit and ponder. Even the words he thinks he recognizes alter as soon as he shifts his stare, spawning new letters and swallowing old, as if this was not paper but a square of forest floor, bursting with fecund and ravenous life.

Of course, he thinks: of course! By *these* means – by *this* device – Henderson will tell all. It is clearly not the knock at the door that DogFellow should fear. He bears the trap in his hairy hand, made into the guileless agent of his own ruin. The noose that will hang him is wrought from ink. But no! DogFellow will not be caught out. Did Henderson, laughing perhaps, imagine it might be done so easily? What a fool he must be –

DogFellow thinks he will go down to the sea at once. Go down to the sea and drown it, paper, words, laughter, lies and all. Then he thinks otherwise, hatching a better plan, for in its current quicksilver flight from idea to idea his brain is altogether excelling itself. And this is what DogFellow decides he must do: he will eat the paper that Henderson intends to be handed in, and by this expedient destroy the power of the word to destroy him.

Moving as swift as is seemly, he seeks out the quiet of his own hut, meeting only two or three along the way, and they turn aside as soon as they see him. There is no time to delay. He lets the door-flap drop and stands for a moment, feeling the texture of the paper, rubbing at it. How many pages? Not so many; two or three chapters at most, a mere fragment of the mysterious whole. Carefully he squats, cross-legged, the manuscript now in his lap. The only noise is the noise of blood rushing through his veins and heart. He lifts the first page as if it were a wafer and nibbles at the edge. It softens and breaks between his teeth. There is little flavour, just a curious pulpy sensation moving between his misshapen molars and across his tongue. Emboldened, he bites again and again. There is a tearing sound. He bites a third time, a fourth, a fifth, feeding in the last two inches with his finger ends. He chews as hard as he is able, mashing it to a spongy mass and swallowing. It reminds him of badly prepared stew, though this is empty of any consolation. There is only a creeping bitterness and the sensation of something clotted and heavy dragging through his gullet. The second sheet is crumpled into a ball and stuffed whole into his mouth. He chews and chews, pauses for a few moments, and then chews some more, until the pap is fit for swallowing. Eight – nine – ten times more he's put to these exertions and still it isn't finished. If only he had a little sugar to sprinkle on!

Towards the end it becomes more than a little awkward. He thinks he will heave it all up, letting loose once more those incriminating words, with their dreadful power to slanderize him. He perseveres, however, gulps hard, keeps it down, and is at last done. Whatever was writ upon the page has been annihilated, as if it had never been: the ink sucked back into Henderson's pen, the laughter crammed back into his mouth. Now let it be his turn to swallow –

Finished, DogFellow sighs with relief, gets up, rubs his belly, and is already halfway out of his hut when the question of what he is to say to the Master rises like a spectre into his mind: nothing, of course, nothing; if he is asked, he will answer . . .

'Nothing.'

The Master, who is holding a large fragment of cranium as if it were an outsize piece of turtle egg, clucks his tongue in sheer annoyance. He has come out from his laboratory. There is blood on the bone, and a few strands of black hair. DogFellow stands at the threshold, solemn, sorry that he must be the bearer of such vexatious news.

'Nothing at all?'

'No, Master.'

'What on earth is he playing at, God damn it?'

DogFellow is ready to answer with something when, with a shake of the head, the Master turns and kicks the door shut with his heel.

Twenty-four

His stomach hurts and his toilet habit is more than usually prolonged. He squats in the woods, not far from the shore, and groans out loud, arching his invisible tail, holding his neck rigid, and pointing his snout skyward. He may piss like a man, but he shits like a dog, despite his best efforts.

Afterwards, when he has finished, he looks it over and he sees how the paper has been rendered down, so that there might never be any recovery of its constituent parts, not even so much as a single solitary letter: the blackness is gone, leeched out during its labyrinthine transit through his innards. It might be undigested pith that he is looking at, or the denatured remnants of some excessively fibrous breakfast. Whatever the words and thoughts by which Henderson hoped to snare him, they are no more.

He digs his heels into the earth and kicks backwards, surrendering to a frenzy of leg action. When it passes, and he peers behind himself, there is nothing left to see beyond a patch of turned soil. The act is done. Why, then, the feeling that something terrible still has to be passed? Slowly, with an aching rump, he turns about and goes back towards the house.

The Master wakes a little after five. It has not taken him very long to return to his old habits. He puts on his shirt and runs a brush through his silver hair and across his grey beard, sparing a glance in the bedside mirror as he does so. Seized by a queer urge he grimaces at his reflection, pouting his lips and then drawing them suddenly back to expose his good teeth.

'Old ape,' he mutters, and in this odd humour he wanders through to his study. Everything is as it should be: the serried ranks of hide-bound books; the faded, steel engravings of Owen, Linnaeus, Buffon and Lamarck; a map of the world thirty years out of date; the presentation stethoscope mounted on the varnished plinth, its incised copperplate dedication still sharp. On his desk there are more books, a fox's skull and the calendar, left where he dropped it, showing this month, with the twenty-fifth day circled by a double loop. On the faintly waxy paper the ink is still a little wet, as is the exclamation mark he set next to it, a reproach to his own unprecedented forgetfulness. He picks up the handbell that sits next to his blotter and gives it a vigorous shake. Moments later, and there is a tentative knocking at the half-open door.

'Come in,' he says.

DogFellow enters.

'I want some tea.'

'Yes, Master.'

'Don't make it too strong. Two spoons for the pot. You made it too strong yesterday.'

DogFellow turns to go.

'Was that you earlier?'

'Master?'

'I thought I heard some noise in the kitchen. Were you making supper?'

'Yes, Master.'

'So what's it to be this evening, hm?'

DogFellow is at a loss what to answer. Fortunately, the Master is not really interested in anything that DogFellow has to say.

'Surprise, is it? Very good. Now hurry along. I'm thirsty. And two spoons only. That's quite enough.'

Back in the pantry DogFellow crams wood into the stove and heaves a sigh of relief, glad that the Master let things pass. Since he came back from the beach – all afternoon in fact – DogFellow has worked. As if to remind himself, he steals a sniff at his own fingers and catches the mingled reek of the dozen substances he ground together in the big mortar. It must have been the noise from this that the Master heard, even though DogFellow was painfully delicate in his ministrations, wrapping the club-end of the pestle in cloth and working the mixture grain by grain, milling everything down with stealthy exactitude.

He had taken what he needed from the bottles on the high shelf in the laboratory, clambering up on a box balanced across a chair. It was not easy to do, but he managed, going up and down very slowly, thinking only on his plan and nothing else. Of course, if he had slipped, or let a jar drop from his grasp to strike the chair edge and break against the floor; or if the Master had been flushed out of his post-meridian slumber and come storming down the corridor, then there would have been more than mere trouble. He need only consider poor Hector, in the infirmary with heatstroke, to see what might befall. But DogFellow kept his head clear, just as he kept his hands – which never sweat – rock steady, and so the Master slept on.

He must be allowed it: allowed to lie recumbent, his white skin against the white sheets. Those other beast people do not think he ever rests, think that he exists instead in a permanent state of divine wakefulness, either working as a god works, at the business of making life, or else watching, as gods do, present like the breath of the sea in the all-about air. They do not even think (the simpler sort at least) that he has clothes as they do, which can be put on and taken off. DogFellow alone sees and understands, and is sensitive to the terrible burden such understanding entails. The god must rest. The god is possessed of flesh, which, while magnificent in its solidity, is still as vulnerable as DogFellow's own tawny hide; and because of this, for this reason above all others, Dog-Fellow has decided that Henderson must die.

But how to achieve it? Knife, club, gun? No, none of these. DogFellow is not strong enough. He knows he could never strike the American down. Stealth and guile are DogFellow's weapons; in this he has applied himself. He can remember exactly how Henderson wolfed down the twist of sugar left out in the woods; the way it was tipped in an eye blink into his gaping mouth and greedily eaten, every last speck. Therein lies the means to accomplish what DogFellow would do. Stealth and guile have led him to it. He lets his imagination run forward, picturing the scene. He again sees Henderson in his mind's eye, coming out to pick up the fold of paper; sees how, once more, the sugar is devoured, the paper licked clean; only now pleasure is succeeded by a moment's shocked surprise and then sudden, fiery pain, worse even than the knife in the mouth. First Henderson chokes and then, clutching his throat, topples forward, to gasp and writhe on the forest floor, his own poisonous tongue turning black –

DogFellow nods, well satisfied by his plan, and prods at the fire in the stove with a stick. Getting the sugar to bait the trap presented no difficulties; he is the cook after all, with free access to the big tin casks in which all the kitchen condiments are kept. Even while the Master snored away (or while perhaps he dozed, half wondering, half oblivious to the muffled noises coming from some corner of the house), DogFellow effected the penultimate part of his plot, putting three, four, five tablespoons of sugar into the mortar, momentarily burying his own mix. Then with a spatula he turned the grains over and over, watching as the pristine white crystals took on a greyish pallor. He paused at this, his certitude momentarily knocked off-centre. Yet in the forest it is dim, and Henderson will want only to eat – to gorge himself on this bounty.

DogFellow does not know exactly what it is that he has made, and might no more guess at its chemical composition than unravel a line of hieroglyphics, yet the Master has warned him often enough that to taste even a dab of any part of his pharmacopoeia is to bring on irredeemable suffering and certain extinction. What then might ten – twenty – fifty times that amount do? He shuts his eyes and once more jumps forward, picturing Henderson sprawled out on the floor of the forest. The American's body twitches once, twice, and then, with a terminal rattle, subsides into the leaf litter and fades away. With the liar die the lies, and the Master may sleep, with DogFellow standing watch over him.

The mixture that's been made now lies in a bottle, corked and stowed out of sight under a loose floorboard by the door of the infirmary. Tonight will surely be the last night the Master who is not a Master will ever spend on the island.

'What's this?'

'It is parrotfish, Master,' says DogFellow.

'You gave it to me yesterday.'

DogFellow steps back from the table.

'Yes, Master.'

'So it is hardly a surprise, is it now?'

'No, Master.'

'Tsk!'

DogFellow, aware that he has got off lightly, prepares to retreat.

'Just a moment.'

DogFellow stops. The Master sips at a spoonful and wrinkles his nose at its piscine blandness.

'Pass the pepper.'

As he shakes the black powder over the surface of his food he says, 'You must be getting forgetful. Don't recall what it is you're giving me. It won't do. In this heat, anything left out, anything not prepared and eaten on that day . . . you want me laid out, do you? Germ theory – pathways of infection – we must be on our guard. It would help if you started writing things down, making little notes. You know . . . what d'you call it – draft a menu. You could manage that, just about. Perhaps we could have a couple of lessons. Turn you into a regular maître d'. What do you think?'

In truth, what DogFellow thinks is of no relevance or importance whatsoever in the scheme of things; the question is little more than a reflex, tagged on to the end of the usual table talk. Yet while he is no more capable of producing a menu than he is of riding a bicycle, DogFellow does grasp the meaning of the word 'lessons', and his heart swells accordingly.

'Still,' continues the Master, 'if I were honest I would admit I too am guilty of the occasional lapse. No doubt the tribulations I've been put to of late have played their part . . .' He pauses to shake his head – a moment's concession to grief over his lost shirts. Then: 'I found out I am a week out in my reckoning; have been all month. I completely forgot that van Toch will be here the day after tomorrow.'

The swollen heart sputters, reverses current and begins to pound.

The Master – indifferent, unknowing – slurps up a spoonful and nods.

'That's better. Pepper makes all the difference. The magic ingredient. Mmm. Of course, you'll have to make yourself useful. Put everything in order. He's bringing me five new specimens; at least he's promised me. Two more big cats, some sort of monkey, a pregnant sow and oh – it nearly slipped my mind – a canine of uncertain origin. Company for you, eh?'

And he peers at DogFellow through the steam that is rising off his bowl.

Twenty-five

The next morning he is set to task, putting the cages together, assisted by Lemura and Handy. Everything goes terribly slowly, and there is a confusion of nuts and bolts tipped into the dirt, so that when the Master appears a little before noon he is very displeased to see what little progress they have made.

'You are all of you hopeless!' he rages. 'I never saw such incompetence. Why has that hammer been left lying there like that? What's this by my foot? Say if the cargo was ready to be unloaded, what would I be able to do? Tell Captain van Toch to take another turn about the ocean while we waited for you pudding-heads to put all the screws in order? Well?'

DogFellow, obliged to take on the burden of responsibility, mumbles his apologies.

'All right, all right,' says the Master tersely. 'Fortunately for you I'm not expecting the ship until tomorrow, by which time you might just have finished . . . well, just make sure you are, or I'll have your hides.'

Still grumbling, he leaves the yard, and the hapless workers continue their struggle with the spanner and the iron frames.

'Time to eat,' says Handy, after a while. The rattle of the dinner bell is already beginning to fade away.

'No. We work,' says DogFellow.

Lemura and Handy exchange doleful glances. 'But –'

'No buts, you lazy scoundrels. We work!'

In his intonation and his mien DogFellow does a more than passable imitation of the Master. The others are cowed and dare not protest further. It is only as the dinner bell sounds again for supper that their task nears completion.

'We can eat now?' asks Lemura tentatively.

DogFellow surveys the row of cages lined up against the wall.

'Yes,' he says, then adds, 'You go first. The Master and me, we have to talk.'

The others nod and creep away. Alone, DogFellow studies his hands. They are steady, without the ghost of a tremor. He has hardly slept since yesterday, but he is not tired. He looks to his left, to where the tin door of the infirmary lies slightly ajar. His poison sugar is there, waiting. To fetch it – to leave it, for *him* to eat – that would be easy enough. Any other course must prove dangerous and unsure. And yet –

The impulse to do the other thing is sudden and irresistible. Let Henderson take his boat; let him depart forever. Let it all be restored, as it was before. Let it be done, and done now.

Quickly he walks out through the gate. He does not feel afraid. His resolve lies like a hand about his heart, holding it steady. As he walks he meets no one. They are all at the House of Food: the unwitting, at their eating.

Back in his hut, in silent seclusion, he stoops and digs in the corner, finding the box that is his secret store. He brushes off the dirt, undoes the string, lifts the lid and takes out the precious two-inch pencil stub which he found in the trash. With a shard of stone selected for the purpose, he carefully scrapes off a little of the yellow wood that guards the lead. For paper he will use a jagged triangle of brown paper, sequestered from the Master's stores months before.

Already, the light is beginning to fade, made worse by a drift of grey cloud moving across the face of the dipping sun. It is too dim for him to see properly. He must go back outside. He puts pencil and paper into his pocket and as coolly as he can – as if, in fact, he were playing the part he takes in his nightly dreams and daytime reveries, strolling through the boulevards and parks of Paris – he passes along the path, sampling the evening air.

He does not travel towards the fields, but walks as if he intended to return for dinner, or even to the compound. His tongue twitches in his mouth, rehearsing the pleasant excuses he will serve up should any nosy beast person dare to ask where he is going, but no one greets him.

The truth is, there have been far better evenings, for the breeze is up, and there is a taste of something on the air. DogFellow hardly notices. His attention is fixed on the best way to leave the track and get in amid the bushes that shade this part of the way. Looking quickly left and right he takes his chance and moves in among the leaves and branches, grateful as they enfold him.

He presses forward as far as he can and stops, hunkering down, cocooned by foliage. No passer-by might see him. He rests the paper on his knee and takes the pencil in his left hand. He holds it with difficulty, its thin stem trapped between his thumb and first two fingers. He contemplates the paper's wrinkled surface as the Master might contemplate skin before making a first incision. The whirr of a bird flying overhead breaks the spell. The light is going. If it is truly to be done, he must begin.

Breathing slowly through his nose, he sets the pencil tip to the top edge of the makeshift page. He starts to press down, and at the same time eases his hand back towards himself. The dark line, betraying the slightest wobble, unspools itself: unspools and unspools, with a sudden acceleration that catches DogFellow out, and he's suddenly swerved off the paper, leaving a senseless squiggle in his wake. Wincing in irritation, he waits for a moment and bunches himself up, trying perhaps to gain a better purchase over his own wayward self. He turns the paper over and begins again. Hand tensed, he positions his pencil an inch below the ragged top edge and this time dares a quick, vertical dash. His mark shows itself bold and dark. Hardly daring to move again he lifts the pencil and now strikes sideways, catching the top of the first line exactly as he knows he must. He breathes out and sees:

T

Moving his wrist a fraction to the right he repeats the first gesture, shaping another vertical, except this time he does not break when he reaches the foot of the line, but doubles back instead, if only for an instant, before letting the pencil ride outwards and then drop. The gesture is near fluent, though at the end the compulsion to swerve off almost masters him, and he has to concentrate supremely in breaking free. He gazes at what he's made, recognizing it, and the sound it makes:

h

He is perspiring, despite the cooling wind that brushes against his face, even in this thicket. If only it were finished now! Yet he has merely begun.

With aching hand and his heart in his mouth, he makes another letter and another: first an 'e', then an 's' (which tortures him with its devious curves), another 'h', an 'i', and then a 'p', which tricks him by its alphabetical kinship with q, and so he presents it as its twin.

Blinking the sweat out of his eyes, and conscious that there are beast voices riding on the air, he writes the next word: *c*, *o*, *m*, *e* and (again treacherous, treacherous!) *s*. He breathes a sigh of relief, only to suck it in again – his bold hand has been a little too much that way, and there is scarcely space left for another letter, let alone the quantity that must follow. He is perplexed, yet he is not defeated. Shrewd and clever – the cleverest beast person by far – he draws an arrow where the next *t* might go and, reversing the paper once more, sets this *t* down, and another *o* and *m* and then –

They are almost on top of him, no more than a yard away. Their laughter is so open and loud he is sure that they have discovered him. In a panic, he lets the pencil drop, while stuffing the paper inside his shirt. But they have not realized that he is there, cowering in the brush.

'My turn now!' squeals one, trying to wrest the pebble from the other's grasp. DogFellow identifies the back of Ebor's legs: the scars run so deep down the calves that each looks like an elongated pair of buttocks. Ebor's playful growl rumbles overhead: 'No, it's mine,' he says, and runs on; the other – DogFellow is not sure who – yields to another squeal and races after.

Still alarmed, DogFellow gets awkwardly to his feet. His consternation is tempered by a censorious impulse, that two beast people should be out at this time, playing stupid games. The paper is against his chest. He looks down but can't see the pencil. He expends a few futile moments in searching, but then yields to the inevitable and creeps out. The other two have vanished; without trying to see where, he walks on, not too fast, not too slow, first towards the beach and then to the east.

In the dullness of the forest he pulls out his message and he reads it once out loud before putting it in the accustomed place. No one hears him, save perhaps the birds, but their language is not his language, nor are his words theirs.

The ship comes tommo

Hoping that Henderson at least will understand, he turns and leaves the trees behind him.

228

The woods were alive in entirely new ways: alive with soft hooting and the shadowed movement of bodies among the branches. A throaty mewling might be heard, or the unabashed puff-pant of some transaction, perhaps wending its way to an ear-splitting climax, or else dissolving into a babble of mutual gratification given and received. It was because of all this activity that he did not at any point pause as he passed down the forest paths, which his feet alone now followed. He would wake up a little before dawn and, after washing himself in a bowl of water gathered the night before, go down to the beach to wait: this sequence of actions became a justification in its own right, like a stick carried between the teeth – something he could feel, something to remind him of what was, of what is.

'*Ooooo – ooo – ooooh –*'

The sound, an elongated suspiration without meaning or sense, came from a bush which pressed so close to his right arm that the new buds on its stems prodded his flesh. Confining himself to a theatrical snort of disgust he hurried past, but he could not resist a sly sideways glance through the leaves and the lattice of soft growth, to see a naked back, and one, two, three hands caressing dappled skin. He looked away instantly, feeling shame at his own weakness, and pretended that there was only the path in front of him, although it was itself difficult to make out through the blur of encroaching greenery. And once more, before he broke free from the tree cover, he was made conscious of movement, soundless this time, yet vigorous enough to send a crop of saplings into a sustained fury of quivering. He held his breath for the final half-dozen yards and surfaced on the beach like a dolphin, blowing hard and gulping in the sea air as if it were a purifying draught. He was much relieved to find that there were no signs of any beasts along the strand, nor any indication that they had been there recently. If he kept his back to the wall behind him he need only watch the play of the ocean and the vault of the sky, with birds the sole other living things to put up with, and that was easy enough to bear.

He had learned to stop thinking about forgetting, to even stop thinking about remembering, on the principle that each renewed attempt to rifle through the store of what he knew was a diminishment, a wearing out of its substance, just as the repeated handling of his precious scrap of newspaper had taken its toll. It was enough to know that the broad paths through the park, and the elegant gentlemen and beautiful ladies were all nearby, immured in his mattress. By the same token, inside the fastness of his curiously shaped skull, tucked away in some curve or corner, lay everything that mattered, safe from the anarchy of island life.

He focused only on the far line of surf as it beat against the atoll and for the first time he noticed that only after every fifth or sixth attempt did the surge gain power enough to engulf the coral and sweep across its stony lip into the lagoon. In between times there was not sufficient momentum, and the waves shivered apart, spilling backwards with a confused and seething motion, perfectly audible in the still air of morning. After a while he allowed the ceaseless rhythms of the water to catch and lift him, so that at first he bobbed on this near side of the atoll, as weightless as a gob of spume, and then, suddenly, he was drawn up and clear above the rushing surface of calcified stone and out, on to the expanse of the Pacific itself. He felt no fear, no desire, nothing at all, until his inner demon roused him to look, look, not out across the infinite blue, but down, into water tinctured red, and he saw, in the depths, his two Masters, looking back up at him –

He was there, on his haunches, alone. Galvanized, he glanced to his right, to where the house still stood, looking from this distance as monumental and whole as ever it did. DogFellow muttered some formulation of his own invention – a prophylactic against angry gods – and got to his feet. He felt the weakness of his own words. Whatever is buried will be uncovered; whatever sinks must rise up . . .

He was agitated now, not knowing whether to stay or to go. He could not bear to return through the forest, nor to stay where he was, and so he took a leftward path along

231

the sand, which was clean and dry and showed no trace of beast or booted foot. Yet he had not expended a minute in his agitated pacing before he stopped again and snuffled the air. The smell was unmistakable and so evocative that he felt his innards contract while his mind dilated, back to the brief horror of his sea vision and back further, to the deserted house and its putrid freight –

Was this real? The foul metal taste on his tongue would not go away, nor the odour. He dared to go a few paces further, towards the boulder that rested at the juncture where sea and sand mingled, and the closer he got the stranger things became, and he saw how the black surface of the basalt was not constant, but pulsed with vitality, filling the stillness of the beach with a dull rasping noise. The smell grew more pungent, coming on in a renewed gust, like the waves he had been watching, and it became almost material, a kind of wadding or gauze, steeped in decay and jammed against his face.

At his foot there was a fallen coconut. He stooped to pick it up and then, as best as he could, he tossed it at the blackness. His aim was not awry and instantly the mob of flies lifted up, showing the body beneath. DogFellow closed in, but not directly; instead he walked up the beach a little, circling what he had found. For a few moments he was possessed by the most dreadful notion that somehow this was the coda to his nightmare and the sea had spewed up the dead, until he understood that it was an impossibility, for the house still stood, and the house was locked, and besides, besides, this thing – broken, stinking – had, by every indication, once been a beast person.

Given renewed courage, he dared to walk within a couple of yards of it. The face was turned aside, half buried in sand, and no scrap of clothing remained. Yet by the bulbous head and abnormally elongated arms which rested in parallel with the torso DogFellow knew that it was Slope. Already the flies had returned, encasing the discoloured flesh and heaving thickest about the ferocious welts that criss-crossed Slope's naked shoulders. These were not the signs of ancient surgery, freshened up by the teeming assault: some other force, some clawed hand or unsheathed tooth, had ripped poor Slope's hide.

Oh Master, Master, see what they do?

And DogFellow returned his gaze to the horizon, hoping for a sign, receiving nothing. In dismay he retreated up the beach a hundred yards and sat down. He did not want to leave poor Slope lying there, to be rendered down to tatters and bones, although he had not got strength or stomach enough to excavate a grave and pile stones on top. The thought of setting hands on the fly-blown remains was too much to bear. In the end he went back to the fringes of the forest and found a piece of wood, long enough and sturdy enough for his purposes. With one end of it he first swatted away the flies, which arose once more in a humming cloud. Then, manoeuvring carefully, he wedged the same end under Slope's ribs and, with a levering action, he turned the body over and over again. It was as solid and unyielding as the wood itself, and he was sure that whatever Slope had been in his inmost self – whether this self was brought into being at the edge of a surgeon's knife, or possessed some other, older provenance

– it was now no more, having gone away, perhaps like a morsel of foam on the back of the ocean.

DogFellow got the body out on to the wet sand and rolled it further out, so that the water lapped about the wounded back and then broke gently over the upturned face, with its tiny eyes screwed shut.

'Goodbye, friend,' said DogFellow, and he remembered the little shrimps they once fished for, as Slope was borne out by one final push, and then sank slowly from view.

Twenty-six

The next morning, as they gather to tender their responses, shouting out against the tearing and the pressing of the flesh, DogFellow feels the first dab of rain fall against his face. Afterwards the beast people disperse to eat their breakfast and go their several ways, while he passes through the gates to where the empty cages lie, awaiting the creatures that will come, perhaps today, or perhaps tomorrow. He tends to little tasks, such as can be performed without thinking, which is as well because the inside of his head is otherwise occupied, and from time to time his body seems co-opted into some imaginary scenario, and the broom he carries moves in tandem with a hidden drama.

He sees with his inner eyes a figure running down the strand, his feet flickering silently, while all the while the Master stands talking to the Dutchman, utterly oblivious, and then with a quick splash this man is in the water and in another two ticks he is aboard the boat itself, slipping over the side and hiding under a tarpaulin, ready to sail away for ever and ever and ever. Better this way than any other, because nothing of him will remain on the island, and the Master does not know, does not understand, while by the time van Toch discovers his stowaway it will be too late, far too late, to turn back –

DogFellow is just picturing Henderson back home in America, back home in Paris, when, with a thump of boots against boards, the Master appears in the doorway. He has his hands in his pockets; his unlit pipe waggles between his teeth. He looks approvingly at the way the dirt has been combed over.

'Nice work,' he says.

Brought out of his alternative world, where everything is fraught, DogFellow is conscious now of only the Master's gaze and, after a few moments, of the smell of burning tobacco. He finishes off one corner and begins over again, following the fine lines he has already made. This is how it ought to be, always, and how it will be, from now on –

'You missed a bit,' he is told, though not in an admonitory way. 'Look, behind you. See?'

Whether he sees or not is of no consequence to Dog-Fellow; the patch is scrubbed, and then smoothed down. Daring to glance over, he sees the Master smile at him before returning his attention to his pipe bowl.

'Good,' he murmurs.

DogFellow shivers with pleasure and wishes the yard was ten times the size so that he might have most of it still to clean, but the morning is wearing on, and besides, how much praise can the loyal heart take?

The Master cocks one eye skyward.

'Don't think the weather will hold, though. Bloody nuisance, given Captain van Toch's reluctance to sail on anything that doesn't have the complexion of a millpond. Still, we live in hope, eh, lad?'

DogFellow, recognizing that these words pertain in some way to matters of the greatest moment, tries and fails to understand.

'Well, we'll see.'

And he goes back into the house, to whatever it is he is doing.

An hour later, and the rain has begun to fall in earnest. DogFellow withdraws to the side of the house, reluctant to go in, unwilling to put himself out of earshot of any ship's horn or distant clanking engine. He looks inside his head and this time sees the cave where Henderson crouches, perhaps by a fire, perhaps in the dark. How will Henderson know if van Toch comes or not? What if he has not found the message or, if he has found it, what if he has failed to take the meaning of the words, thinking that the marks left are nothing but stray squiggles or a pattern left by dirty bird feet? DogFellow feels panic rise up in his chest. He grips the staff of the broom to steady himself. The notion that Henderson should fail to seize this chance and leave the island is more than he might bear. No, he tells himself, no. The ship will come, and Henderson – Henderson will depart. And, repeating this over and over, he watches as the rain turns all his morning's labours to sodden muck.

But the next day is no better, nor the next. The Master has him indoors, greasing all available metal surfaces against the threat of rust. He likes it best when he has charge of some bladed implement, and he must guide his slippery fingers with extreme care, so as not to nick himself: by these means he is compelled to forgo his imagined pictures of Henderson, either squatting in ignorance or else performing his sprint across the sand, and concentrate on avoiding the glittering edges of surgical and kitchen knives, and the scissors (a dozen pairs) which the Master feels obliged to keep about the place. It is when he languishes that he is lost, and a score of times he fights with the need to run into the woods, to see if his message still lies where he left it.

Once, he hears what he takes to be the forlorn wail of the coming boat, riding the wet air like whale song, and dares to lay off his current job (greasing the Master's boots by now) to go down to the gate. There is nothing to see, except the high-headed waves of the Pacific running hard against the shore, and he gets drenched into the bargain. Perhaps it was a whale, calling out to the land, seeing the grey hummock of the house and growing lovesick at the sight. DogFellow feels a moment's pity for the creature, echoing his own miserable frustration. Then he shakes himself and, with a sneeze, runs back indoors.

Squat on the floor, his hair still damp, he holds the Master's left boot in both hands and turns it over, letting the supple leg flop sideways. It is now so shiny black that he can see his own reflection, pulled long and solemn over the contour of the foot. The shallowness of his forehead –

a constant source of embarrassment for him – now appears corrected to something like a regular width, and if he tips his head forward a fraction, it even begins to wax high, lofty and distinguished . . .

In Paris, in Unitedstates, in that curious metropolitan hybrid he has concocted out of the two, he will look just like this, and he will wear fine clothes, and bear a silver-capped stick, and wear these kind of boots, or better even, because the one he holds has a patch in its sole, and the seams are starting to bare their crossed stitches. He glances across at his own naked, ugly feet, stretched out in front of him, and he makes them disappear, seeing instead what he wants to see, though only for an instant, because then he is looking at Henderson, standing on the deck of the *Kangdong Bandoeng* and reaching out his hand to scrub the top of his companion's head, as they sail away, away . . .

With a grunt he hits his leg, striking out that particular image, and the chain that follows.

No, no!

Henderson must go, yes, of course, but he, DogFellow, he will stay, he will remain – and as if in response the Master appears, still with the pipe he has nursed through all this wet weather, a little tired with waiting for the ship that will bring him new things to cut and to make, yet in all other respects surprisingly well disposed towards a world he normally views askance, even on hot days.

'It occurs to me,' he says, picking up on a conversation he has been having with himself for the past five minutes, 'that I've been a little remiss in your own improvement recently.'

He puts his pipe in his mouth, sucks on it, takes it out again and looks quizzically into the smoulder-free bowl.

'By which I mean, having you – having you . . .'

He loses himself in the close inspection of his dottle, but DogFellow has already guessed what will come next. The scar tissue at the root of his back starts to twitch.

'So: shall we get to our books?'

The last word is a benison, falling on him as the rain falls upon the roof, but sweeter by far. He carefully puts the boots away and eagerly follows the Master into another part of the house.

Twenty-seven

'*Liar!*'

What was that?

DogFellow's ears, ever acute, catch the sound, coming as if from far away.

It occurs again, a little louder:

'*Hoi! Lii-aaa-rrr!*'

But the Master, it seems, is oblivious to this invocation. He continues to sit, waiting for DogFellow to say what he sees set out on the page in front of him.

Another noise follows, quick on the heels of the last – not a cry, this time, but the sound of wood striking wood, a dull thud vibrating through the still, damp air. Five days have gone by and still the ship has not come. The day before the rains eased at last, at first to a scatter of occasional showers and now to nothing at all, though the skies have not properly cleared.

DogFellow stares dry-mouthed at the pictures in front of him and at the words stacked underneath.

'Hmm?'

The Master is not impatient, yet he is quietly urging DogFellow to begin deciphering the black clusters, to tell the story of the boy and his faithful companion. Dog-Fellow swallows and begins to raise his tongue.

'*God damn –*'

There is no denying it. The voice is as clear and sharp as a pinprick. No longer able to participate in the Master's studied concentration, he lets his eyes slip off the page.

'Never mind that,' says the Master. 'Give your attention to this.'

And one strong white finger – whiter than the page it apostrophizes – shows him what he ought to be focusing on. So the Master has heard too. DogFellow bows his head a little and begins.

'Tom throws the ball, and Rover runs . . .'

The gates, which haven't been fastened, swing open with a clatter. The Master does not take his hand off DogFellow's shoulder, nor give any outward sign of perturbation. DogFellow, however, who has been clumsily enunciating the sentences before him, allows the latest syllable to die against his teeth as he cranes his head sideways towards the door.

'*God damn it, you dirty cheat –*'

It is Henderson, here, now: Henderson, tossed between high dudgeon and high fever, come down at last from the headland where he has been camped out for six drenched days, with nothing now to lose in his own addled estimation.

'*– where's – my – frigging – boat!*'

He has waited all he can, feeding off hope, off a scrap

of paper with its imbecile scrawl, but now he will wait no longer.

'Cheats, cheats, cheats!'

'Finish the page,' says the Master, and DogFellow – who should by rights be frightened, for what is to happen now? – draws strength and boldness from the weight of that hand, and the calm invincibility of that presence, and resumes his infant's narrative, of the ball and the boy and the beloved animal friend who is the boy's constant companion.

'Where the hell are you, you son of a –'

Further down the house there is a violent crash and the tinkle of broken glass. The Master grunts in annoyance. He says, 'That is all for today,' and reaching over Dog-Fellow's shoulder he folds the book shut.

A second crash, still louder, is heard: Henderson is kicking at the door.

'Hoi!' he yells. His voice cracks with emotion. 'I want to talk to you!'

Without another word to DogFellow – without telling him either to stay or to go – the Master walks out into the corridor, pauses for a moment, and then strides down to confront this unprecedented disturbance. Left alone, all DogFellow's control disappears and his terror is immediate and boundless: why has Henderson come here, with his threats and his treacherous speaking? To DogFellow's way of thinking he should be waiting – waiting –

'You no-good, cheating charlatan, stop hiding –'

Wanting only the comfort of the Master's proximity, DogFellow goes out just as the key is turned. He sees him in profile, the grey light of the overcast afternoon falling on him through the open doorway.

'And you will tell me what you mean by coming here and creating such a disturbance?'

His timbre brooks no contradiction. It makes Dog-Fellow's heart turn over as he scuttles to be at his Master's heels. Henderson, who has retreated to the middle of the yard, glares at them both.

'I have come,' he says, 'because we have things to discuss.'

'Discuss? Is that a joke? If I didn't know better I'd say you had been drinking again. Look at you, for heaven's sake. You're a disgrace!'

Peeking between the starched white columns of the Master's betrousered legs, DogFellow can see how much worse Henderson has become, with his clothes – such as survive – hanging on him in dirty rags. His beard and hair look utterly wild, and one of his eyes, succumbing to tropical infection, has closed over altogether. But right now there is a desperate energy in the way he is standing, fed by the sickness coursing through his blood, and in his hand he has a large and jagged lump of pumice.

'Just go away. Go on, away with you. Get out of my sight,' says the Master.

'Oh no: no, no, no, no. Not so easily,' says Henderson. 'We have our contract, don't you remember?'

'Whatever accommodation we may have reached has lapsed. You failed to give me what I wanted.'

DogFellow, who is afraid and yet, in the Master's presence, not afraid, reaches out to clasp at a trouser hem.

'Me!' exclaims Henderson. '*You* had what *you* wanted, and you promised *me*. You promised, *promised*, that when the next ship came –'

'Mr Henderson, the gentlemen's agreement that existed between ourselves was entirely dependent on my receiving and approving a final draft of our manuscript, and this you have failed to do.'

'You lying, two-faced swine!' Henderson's face grows purple, like the sheen on the bell of a stranded jellyfish. 'You want to keep me here forever, don't you? You want me to set down my bones alongside all the animals you've butchered and tortured to death in the name of your sick demented science. I see now – I see what you are. To hell with what you saw me writing. That was nothing to what I have now, what I have in here.'

With a theatrical flourish he points to the side of his head.

'Go and tell it to the trees,' says the Master, and he begins to close the door. DogFellow, quicker to react, pushes himself clear. The rock flies in a straight line and smashes against the outside edge of the frame. The Master pulls back, but too late. His hand covers his face as, soundlessly, he tries to grasp the door handle. Missing it he moves forward a pace or two, brushing past the stricken DogFellow.

'Shut it quickly,' he mutters.

DogFellow has just enough wit to do as he is told, braving the terror of an encounter with Henderson, yet Henderson has already vanished.

DogFellow watches as the Master staggers away in the

direction of his bedroom. He sees the way the blood has splashed the floor, forming a chain of ragged discs – blood, astonishingly red, just as it is in all the creatures that he has made and marred.

The Master is speaking to him, saying something –

'A bowl. Some water. Wadding.'

With legs that seem to have lost all strength, all resilience, DogFellow runs the length of the house, to the place of cuts and stitches. He fumbles hopelessly with the jug and spills water across the table before pouring the rest into a dirty dish. Taking a fist of cotton he returns.

The Master is sitting, not on a chair, but on his haunches. The Master squats. DogFellow is numbed to see the mask of red that has supplanted those familiar and terrible features.

'Can – can you see where I'm injured?'

Even the voice is strange. DogFellow backs away.

'Take the wadding and press against it.'

A bloodied hand is raised, as if to catch at DogFellow's sleeve.

'Quickly. It must be the temporal artery. A splinter from that damned rock –'

DogFellow can see where the wound lies: there is nothing neat or orderly in the way the flesh has been gouged. The blood is flowing freely. DogFellow is put in mind of a stony place he knows away in the forest, covered in moss, where water oozes up, exactly like this.

'What – what is it?'

Blinded, he swings out one arm, knocking the bowl out of DogFellow's hands. It falls to the floor with a clatter.

'DogFellow – DogFellow!'

His own hands run through the spreading puddle, instantly colouring it. His fingers find the dressing, lying sodden in a lump by his left knee. He squeezes it and sets it to his face. In that instant the eyes return, flaring up against the ruddy ruin. Recognition passes through DogFellow like an electrical charge.

'Master . . .?'

But he can say no more, because at that moment the hammering begins. It is the old familiar sound, got by beating iron against iron: the dread tocsin that pulls the beast people from their diverse labours and compels them to come before the Master to receive his word. Today, however, everything has changed.

'Help me –'

Before he can do anything DogFellow is grasped about the back of the neck and the Master is using him as a support, dragging himself up with one arm while the other is pressed against the wall. The thrilling reek of blood is worrying at DogFellow's nose. He almost topples over, but somehow the Master manages to get to his feet, and all the while the air is numbed by the rhythmic bashing of the iron triangle.

'Stop it, you blasted fool,' he mutters, and for a moment DogFellow thinks it is he who stands rebuked before understanding that it is intended for Henderson.

'Damn you, damn you –'

Woozy, the Master moves through the next room and the next, towards the other side of the house. Where his hand touches a chest of drawers – briefly, to steady himself – there is a smear of blood, and blood too marks the last door jamb. Through the window DogFellow can see Henderson striking the triangle with a fury.

'Get away from there!'

The Master's voice regains its old thunder. As he tries to draw the door bolt Henderson gives an inarticulate shout and drops down the iron rod on its short chain. He disappears from view.

'Quick – quickly.'

The Master's fingers do not obey his will, and slip off the bolt handle. He is still bleeding and his shirt is losing all pretence to whiteness.

'Quickly,' he repeats, to himself. Then: 'You, Dog-Fellow.'

Frightened, DogFellow lets out a low whine. With a sudden wrench the bolt snaps back into its guard and the door is pulled open wide enough for the Master to squeeze through. Outside there is chaos. Instead of drawing up in their accustomed orders the beast people have gravitated into loose confederations, or else stand singly. They all stare fixedly, not at the bloody apparition who has appeared on the porch, but at the filthy man in their midst. Henderson has begun to shout at them, to harangue them through chattering teeth, and as he shouts he gesticulates, pointing from one beast to another.

'Listen to me,' he says, 'the time has come for you to end the tyranny you live under! The man you have named the Master – who made you worship him, who tortured and killed your kind, is finished – he's all done in! Back there –' he points towards the silent figure and the stricken

DogFellow – 'he's on his last legs. Soon other men will be arriving here. Now is your chance to rise up – rise up and finish him off. Smash him – end it!'

His gaze darts feverishly from one scarred half-human face to the next.

None replies or makes any move either to run forward to the house or back into the forest.

'Look here,' he exclaims, and he snatches a wooden mattock from out of Hobbs's misshapen hand.

'See, see what you could do?' He swings the tool up and down a couple of times, glancing from Hobbs to those nearest him.

'You, give me that –'

Jasper, who has a whole breadfruit clutched to his chest, is robbed of his prize by the importunate grasp of the Master who is not a Master.

'This is that swine – this is him,' says Henderson with terrible conviction as he tosses the ripe sphere into the air and with one ferocious down-swipe knocks a chunk out of it.

'It's him – you see? See how easy it is?'

They watch as in a frenzy of movement and flying pulp the breadfruit is destroyed. DogFellow, daring to go to the bottom of the porch steps, watches too.

'And that's how it's done,' says Henderson, leaving off his destruction to address Hobbs, who has not moved. 'Now –'

Henderson catches at his wrist and presses the sweaty grip of the mattock against his mottled palm.

'You do it. Go to the man who calls himself your maker. Go and beat him across the head!'

The mattock falls down to the ground.

'What's the matter with you?' shouts Henderson. 'What is it with you, and you, or you?'

He runs over to where BearCreature stands.

'You could crush his skull with a flick of your wrist! What's the matter? What's the matter here?'

He takes them all in with his one glittering, feverish eye: the assemblage of pig-men, the transfigured apes, the indeterminate things, hacked out of nature and sewn together again – he subjects them in turn to his gaze, and he starts up once more, shouting for a rebellion that will end the tyrant's rule over the island.

DogFellow listens and hears again those very words that Henderson had used to make a fool of him. But how can the Master stand there, and allow this?

DogFellow looks over his shoulder and sees that he has left, gone, back into the house. He feels as if the island itself was suddenly adrift or falling through space, the ground tipping off the horizontal, and in a moment he is sure the compound behind him – the trees before him – those who stand and listen – and the furious figure of Henderson too – all, all will start to lean and topple, before sliding into the depths of the encompassing sea.

'Well? Aren't you going to do anything?'

Henderson is entering the peroration, combining words with actions as he circles about, trying to draw every beast person into his plan. None will move, perhaps because they are afraid of this sick, furious man, perhaps because they do not understand his words.

'Right! So that's how it's going to, be, is it? Then I'll show you!'

Stooping to pick up Hobbs's mattock, Henderson strides back towards the house. Panicked, DogFellow turns and rushes back up the steps and in through the door. He can hear Henderson behind him and ahead – ahead he can see the Master, stumbling forward, the loaded shotgun in his hands.

One is blinded by blood, the other by fever. The noise from the gun is deafening indoors.

He howls.

'Will you shut up,' he is told. But when the second shot comes, DogFellow howls louder still.

He left his hut behind for good and moved down to the sea, settling in by a sandy hollow shaded by a solitary palm, which seemed as forlorn as himself. He had his blanket still, and his precious fold of newspaper, and several other things besides, not previously revealed because he'd kept them so well hidden.

There were buttons, sixteen in all (but only two matching) which he had somehow accumulated, unable to see them disregarded, though most came his way as rubbish, plucked loose from lost garments and signifying nothing, except to him. There was sealing wax, and a dozen candle ends, and iron nails, which had been drawn out of packing cases and sequestered in the turn-ups of his trousers. There was string, sedulously collected, with some pieces as short as his little finger and others (a few) nearly as long as himself. There was an old leather glove, far too big for either of his hands, and with a hole in its thumb; but he kept it anyway, because of who it had belonged to, and a certain smell still lingered. There was a sixpenny bit, with *the late Queen's head in profile; a surgical needle, bent in the middle; three empty medicine bottles, with glass stoppers intact; half a spool of silken thread; five sheets of writing paper; and – prize among prizes (next to his scrap of newsprint) – a fountain pen , which he imagined might work, although the nib was splayed beyond recovery, and he had not a drop of ink. No matter: these were his things, and they belonged to him, and he sat by them, hour after hour.*

He was somehow aware, in a vague and peripheral manner, of what he might or even must do, yet for now he felt no urgency, felt very little in fact: the hunger pangs that once had plagued him had departed, and while he didn't care for the way his finger ends could find the hard lines of each and every rib, it was a relief not to be driven by the need to go far off, and spend half the morning scouring the beach and its hinterland for enough to fill his belly. Instead he spent his days listening to himself think, or watching the flight of birds, although his eyes were often sore and a frosted corona spoilt his vision.

Where did they go, he wondered, those birds, with their wings held taut against the still air: they floated against the rival blues of sea and sky, looking down on the island, looking down on him, and then they simply passed away, going off somewhere else, perhaps going home. This exercised him, the mystery of the birds, yet they were finally in themselves mere emblems, a stimulus to other, older thoughts: home, the horizon, and two men, who he began to glimpse not as contrary, or even as different, but as one.

The dead are never dead to those that loved them.

'D-D-Dog –'

He heard a voice and couldn't be sure whether it was in his mind or his ear that the sound lay.

'DogF-F-F –'

He sensed movement behind him and turned to peer at the dark forest. Something moved against the gloom.

'Dog –'

A clumsy mouth repeated the word again.

DogFellow screwed up his face and made out a hunched shape scuttling awkwardly from left to right, like a crab.

'Who is it speaking?' he asked.

A noise, essentially incoherent, did service for a reply.

'Go away,' he said; and he gripped a piece of driftwood and waved it.

'You – you – D-Dog-F-F –'

A creature, bowed down and using its hands as occasional forefeet, drew still closer. DogFellow, who was in truth near-blind from too much sun and sea, waved his stick with greater vigour.

'Keep away!' he cried, and grew frightened at the thin, timorous rattle of his own voice. The creature, covered in sleek brindled hair, halted. For the first time DogFellow could make out that it was completely naked.

'Dog, Dog,' it said, and beckoned at him. 'Come – come –' it panted.

'I stay here,' said DogFellow, shaking his head and pointing his stick at the sand.

'No, you – here – others.'

'I stay,' repeated DogFellow, his voice getting firmer. 'I will not go with you. I will not forget the rule of the cup and the law of the proper two-legged walkers.'

'Come,' said the creature, so close now that Dog-Fellow might see its round, querulous face. 'You – f-f-fff . . .'

DogFellow took a step backwards.

'Keep away. I hate you. You do not know what you are any more.'

'F-forget,' said the creature, and DogFellow raised his stick, as if ready to strike, keeping the posture until he was alone once more.

Later that very day he began to build. He had no clear idea in his head, no plan to work by other than the loosest notion, got up from who knows where: only that if sufficient wood could be gathered and bound together and made fast, with the cracks stuffed and a mast rigged up, it might be made to float, and carry him off and away.

It was not such a concept as came gradually, bit by bit, but was struck up all at once, and DogFellow let himself be swept along by it, as if he already stood upon the creaking timbers, with the swell rising before the breeze, and the birds overhead, pointing the way.

To make the body of it he required the right materials, and while he might ordinarily recoil from the challenge, now his need was such as to trample all over fear and *scruple; so he went to the very shadow of the compound, to scrounge what he could from the general ruin of the palisade.*

The dead eyes of the house were on his bowed head, at his stooped back, while he toiled to drag what he might up the beach, yet he never faltered, even though he was much weaker than he had been, and each step cost him dear in sweat and effort. He was not afraid, because his idea carried all before it, and no sooner had he got the first spars set side by side than the thoughts which possessed him grew still stronger, and he banished his exhaustion and got busy, working with his supply of nails, hammered in with a lump of pumice. It was hard work. The stone fractured, cutting at his palm, and as twilight came he had to stop. Nevertheless, it lay there, in front of him: he had begun his raft.

The next day he went back to gather timber while the house looked on, mute and still. He was not afraid, he told himself, because they were not there, behind the door: they had left, gone away, gone home, passed over the sea, to the place where the birds flew. Popping the sinews across his shoulders, he heaved at a short, thick length of timber, sun-bleached on one side, dark on the other. He dragged it doggedly along, ploughing up the beach, not recogniz-ing that it was the lintel from the fallen gate he held, or not caring: the essence of things had departed, and he'd follow.

As he busied himself, trying to hold each nail exactly straight before pounding at its head, or else resorting to his string, he was aware of being watched, although he did not know by who, or what. He had no time to concern himself any longer.

His raft took shape. It was not what he imagined. Across the unequal sides of the frame he hammered down the flat lengths of wood that comprised the deck. Where gaps appeared, he took his candles and knocked them in sideways on, doing whatever he could. Somehow he was able to jam a dry branch into a knothole, and so he had his mast, with a shorter piece lashed across it, and finally a shred of cloth torn from the hem of his shirt tied at the top, doing service for an ensign.

They watched him as he worked.

Another day passed. DogFellow made himself swallow down coconut milk, although it caused him to gag. He ate a little of the flesh as well, but not too much. The rest he secured, for later: he imagined he might need it out at sea. The bent nail he could not use was tied to a surviving piece of string, and put beside the nut. There'd be plenty of fish to catch, he thought.

As he busied himself, the creature he saw before came back, daring to leave the shadow of the forest. This time he took no notice at all. He saw that there was something that loitered near it; he took no notice of that either.

He rested throughout the latter part of the morning, sleeping soundly for a time, until awoken by a sudden pang of urgency. When he got to his feet his legs felt light, emptied of troublesome sensation. Slowly he began to pull his raft down the slope of the beach. It came easily enough.

He reached the outer skirt of froth and passed through the surf's cream, wading up to his ankles, then up to his knees. He glanced down, but could not see any of the little shrimps.

He felt the raft's light wooden spars lifted by a sudden updraught. The timbers shuddered and creaked, though they held together.

Waist-deep by now, he hauled himself aboard. He was riding a steady current, moving faster than he imagined; there was no time even to be afraid. The shadow of a bird cut across the water in front of him; he tried to look up, and as he looked, the raft turned about, catching an eddy, before being carried clean across the atoll's spine and out on to the restless deep.

Did he still hear a voice? He looked back at the island, lying long and low and green. He listened as hard as he could, and there – it came again.

'DogFellow! DogFellow! Where are you going?'

'To civilization!' he shouted back, and he felt in his pocket for the wet shred of paper.

'To Paris!'

But he was already too far out, and his words were lost.